G000271450

THE MOP & BUCKET MURDERS

A Barney Carmichael Crime Mystery

by

Pat Herbert

Published by New Publications

Copyright © Pat Herbert 2017 First Edition

The author asserts the moral right under the Copyright, Designs and Patents Act 1988 to be identified as the author of this work.

Acknowledgements

My thanks to Darin Jewell for his continued faith in my writing, and to Judith Sturman for her encouragement, advice and support.

She let go of his hand and scrabbled in her handbag for some loose change. She was almost sure she'd had some when she left home that morning, so why couldn't she find any now? If she didn't have a cigarette soon she would explode.

She looked down at her little boy, who was standing patiently by her side. They were outside the newsagents on Brixton High Street, a gentle breeze ruffling the child's hair. She had dressed him so carefully that morning, blue and white sailor suit and matching hat, long white socks and shiny black buckle shoes. He looked a picture, if she did say so herself. The child, being only four, was unaware of the admiring looks he was getting. He wriggled uncomfortably in the clothes that were too hot for him.

It was the last carefree summer before Neville Chamberlain took the country to war. The sun was beating down on the pavements as if it knew no one was going to see it (metaphorically speaking) for six long years. Make the most of it now, it seemed to be saying. But it was too hot for her and she still needed a cigarette.

At last! she thought. She knew she had enough for a packet of ten Woodbines. The shilling had got into the lining of her handbag. It had been fraying for years, her bag, but she couldn't afford a new one. At least, not while she frittered what little money she had on sailor suits for her little boy, not to mention the cigarettes.

"Hello, love," greeted old Chipping, the newsagent. He was sitting behind a pile of newspapers and magazines, looking for all the world like a mischievous gnome. "Hot enough for you?"

"Yes, you can say that again," she said with a weary smile. "Is your daughter not here today?" She knew old Chipping wasn't allowed to serve anymore, owing to his dwindling faculties. He hadn't been able to give anyone the right change for years.

"Yes, she's just getting some stock out the back," replied old Chipping. Nobody ever gave him the honour of a 'Mr' these days. "Sal!" he cackled as loudly as his eighty-seven-year-old lungs would allow. "Customer!"

"All right, Dad. Hold your horses, I can't be in two places at once."

She was desperate for a cigarette now. She even contemplated grabbing old Chipping by his lapels and demanding he hand one over. Luckily, Sally Dawson appeared just then, carrying a large carton of Woodbines. Thank God! she said to herself.

"Hello, Doreen, love," said Sally, grinning all over her chubby face. She looked just like Mrs Bun, the baker's wife, to Doreen. She was the spitting image of her, according to her own pack of cards anyway. All rolls of fat and wobbly jowls, crinkly little eyes disappearing into the folds of her cheeks and an apron straining across her bosom that looked in danger of splitting at any moment.

"Hello, Sally," said Doreen, her hands now shaking from lack of nicotine. "Ten Woodbines, please." She put the money down on the counter. "Just right."

"Just right, love," agreed Sally.

There followed a long wait, however, because Sally had trouble opening the carton. It was all Doreen could do not to lean over the counter and tear at the cardboard with her bare hands. Finally, a packet was extracted from the large box. She had the cigarette out of the packet and alight before Sally Dawson could blink.

"Coo," she said, "you look like you need that!"

"I do. It's been a long day." She puffed away gratefully at the little stub of nicotine.

"You not got Derek with you, then?" asked Sally, leaning over the counter and looking for the little boy.

"Of course, I have. We've been to the library and then to Ferrari's for an ice cream. They do that Rossi's stuff that all the kids love. He got it all over his nice new suit."

"What have you done with him then?" Sally was puzzled.

"He's here, where else would he …." She trailed off. Derek was no longer at her side. She ran out into the street and called his name. There was no sign of him. She started to run up and down the high street, screaming his name now at the top of her voice.

But Derek was gone.

1

Barney Carmichael's detective agency, by rights his and his brother's detective agency, was doing good business these days. Carmichael Private Investigation Services was based in a small, but well-appointed, office on the third floor of a block situated almost opposite the Unilever building on New Bridge Street in Blackfriars. The sun was shining through the window blinds of Barney's office. It had been doing that for most of June and, according to the long-range weather forecast, more of the same could be expected for at least the next couple of weeks.

It was the beginning of the decade which was due to see London swinging by the middle of it. However, in 1961 there was no hint of a movement, let alone a swing. It could have been a decade earlier. Nobody alive and in London had ever heard of the Beatles and, if the male population were to be told that girls would be showing their legs almost up to their bottoms in a few years' time, they would have probably said "nice idea but no chance, mate".

Barney and brother Jim were both in the office that late June morning at the end of a run of interviews. The business was finally doing well enough to employ a secretary; that decision made, it was only left to find the right person. Barney wanted her to be full time, while Jim, ever the more cautious and more fiscally-minded of the two, wanted to try her out on a part-time basis. At least at first.

The last candidate entered the office just as the clock on the wall showed twelve noon. A pretty, trim-looking woman in her mid to late twenties appeared before the two middle-aged men, which was a nice change as most of the other candidates had been older and less prepossessing.

Barney had remonstrated when Jim had complained in the middle of the morning of the lack of female pulchritude on offer. He had also complained that not one of the candidates had been under the age of forty.

"Age is immaterial," Barney had said. "Since when is it a law that a secretary, in order to do her job properly, has to be under twenty-five and pretty? I think good typing skills and a pleasant telephone manner are more important."

Jim had grinned. "Yeah, I suppose so. But a nice pair of legs would also be an asset. For our male clients, anyway."

Barney had agreed reluctantly, secretly wishing himself for a prettier prospect than they had seen so far. Now here at last was Muriel Bird. That's more like it, he thought to himself. As long as she can type and answer the phone with efficiency, the job's hers.

Muriel started working for Carmichael Private Investigation Services the following week. A bright young woman, she had felt suffocated in the shipping office where she had been employed ever since leaving school. She had craved excitement all her young life and had come to the conclusion the shipping office was the last place she would find it. So, in desperation, just to spice up her mundane existence she had married Terry Bird, a young man who had proposed regularly to her once a month for over two years. As he worked in the same shipping office, even if on the floor below, it was difficult to avoid his attentions, so she had finally succumbed. Getting dolled up in white and trotting down a church aisle seemed like a good idea at the time, even though it was mainly just to break the monotony. It wasn't the only reason, as life at home with her nagging aunt was becoming more intolerable as each day passed.

Not that she didn't love her husband. She wasn't stupid enough to swap one intolerable situation for another equally intolerable, but she had found out soon enough he was rather dull. She should have known, of course, as he had been content to sit behind a desk in the shipping office for even longer than she had.

When she informed him she was leaving her safe position in the typing pool, he was horrified. They had been married just over a year and the regular incomes of their two salaries was helping them to save for a place of their own or a baby, whichever came first. Secretly, Muriel was determined that a baby would *not* come first. She wanted a new outlet and changing nappies all day wasn't the kind of outlet she had in mind.

Working in a detective agency, even if it was only in an administrative capacity, involving booking appointments, typing reports and making Barney and Jim endless cups of tea and coffee, was a step in the right direction. Her duties, she was resolved, would change once she had her feet firmly under the desk. She'd show them how indispensable she could be. And she'd also show them that private eyes didn't only come in masculine form either.

So, her first week with Barney and Jim ground slowly on as she got to grips with the awful manual typewriter and the equally awful telephone line that crackled every time she spoke to anyone.

Gazing around the office on her second morning, she could see improvements were much needed. She was a sensible girl, however, and refrained from making too many demands too soon, suspecting that the older generation (which was how she saw Barney and Jim) was resistant to change, especially if it was too radical or, more importantly, too expensive. Still, she thought, she'd soon be able to win them round, fully aware of the power of her feminine charms. She just had to be patient and bide her time. At least she was now in a job that promised the excitement she craved.

Her first week, however, had proved a disappointment to her. There didn't appear to be any interesting cases to solve. Barney had found an erring husband for a worried wife, but it hadn't been too difficult as he had soon been located in the boozer nearest his home. The fact that he didn't want to go back to his wife had been the only bit of excitement in the case, involving Jim and Barney bundling the drunken old man into their car and driving him home. As she typed the resultant report, she began to think that private detective work wasn't all it was cracked up to be.

And, by Friday afternoon of her first week, she suspected the only danger she would be likely to encounter in her new job would be dying of boredom.

2

Inspector Tony Halliday of Scotland Yard was nearing retirement. Thirty years in the force, man and boy, and that was his lot. He had visions in his mind (mainly put there by his wife) of a little cottage in Cornwall where he could spend his autumnal years in peace and contentment. He'd had enough of grisly murder. Growing roses and listening to the birds singing were what he needed now. Get away from it all, away from the terrible things human beings were capable of.

Today, he'd arranged to meet his friend and confidant, Barney Carmichael, in order to get his opinion on another grisly murder he had been lumbered with. An uneasy alliance had grown up between the two men, their paths having crossed on more than one occasion. It is often said that the police regard the independent private detective as nothing but an interfering nuisance, hampering their investigations rather than helping them. However, Barney was a difficult person not to like, and Tony was an easy-going individual who tried to see merit in everybody, even homicidal maniacs.

Their usual meeting place was the Bishop's Finger public house near Smithfield. It was where they had first met, both being drawn by its odd name. They had stayed to share a table and a gut-filling meal of shepherd's pie and apple tart and custard. Today the same menu was on offer.

"Hello, Barney," Tony greeted him. Barney was already seated in an alcove by a side window, their favourite spot whenever it was available. Being a popular pub, however, it was often already occupied if they didn't get there early enough. Today, Halliday was gratified to learn that Barney had made sure of their place by being almost the first person over the threshold when the pub opened its doors at half-past eleven.

"Hello, Tony," Barney responded. "Good to see you. How's tricks?"

"Oh, not so bad," replied Tony Halliday. "Could be worse. Can't stand this heat, though."

"Yes, it *is* a bit much, isn't it?" agreed Barney. "They say it's set to continue."

"It's all right if you don't have to work in it," said Halliday. "Same again?" Barney's half pint was nearly finished, which wasn't surprising as he had been sitting nursing it for almost an hour.

"Er, well, make it a pint this time," said Barney, a sheepish look on his face.

"I've ordered us the usual. Hope that's okay," said Tony when he returned with the drinks.

"Great, thanks. You must tell me what I owe you." He didn't press the point, however.

"You seem a bit down today. And you only had a half just now. Business doing all right, is it?"

"It's okay."

Halliday gave him a quizzical look over his pint.

"Well, I suppose I do have to watch the pennies a bit these days," admitted Barney. "Especially now we've got a full-time secretary."

"A secretary, eh?" Tony gave him a wink as he downed almost half his beer in one go. "What's she like?"

"She seems very efficient."

"No, you chump, what's she like to look at?"

"To look at?"

"Yes, to look at. Have you stopped looking? Are you getting too old to appreciate a pretty girl?"

"Oh, that," said Barney, something obviously distracting him. "Yes, she's okay to look at, I suppose. Jim thinks so, anyway."

Halliday saw there was no point in pursuing the subject. He wanted to know what colour her hair was and what sort of figure she had, but he supposed Barney's own women problems were enough for him. Another female in the mix would probably prove too much. He sipped the rest of his pint slowly as they talked desultorily of inconsequential things, waiting for their food to arrive.

Barney seemed uninterested in what his friend was saying and Halliday was about to try another tack when the shepherd pies finally arrived, courtesy of the pretty barmaid. They sat eating in silence for a while. Halliday, puzzled by Barney's obvious depression, watched him out of the corner of his eye. The shepherd's pie was very tasty but he could see his companion wasn't enjoying it, judging by the way he was moving the food around his plate without attempting to put it in his mouth.

After they had finished their meal, Halliday lit his pipe and Barney drew out a packet of Senior Service. Although he had more or less given them up, he always liked a cigarette after a meal. As they smoked, they studied the clientele around them. The pub was now heaving and very noisy.

"Penny for 'em, old chap," said Halliday at last. "You don't seem your usual chipper self today."

"Oh, sorry, Tony," said Barney, sighing. He stubbed out his cigarette in the ashtray with some force. "I've got a lot on my mind."

"Is business that bad?" Halliday prompted again.

"Oh, no. It's fine. I wouldn't have hired a secretary if that were the case. Jim's a bit fed up with the sort of stuff we're doing at the moment, though. A lot of husband and wife tailing. I always said we wouldn't take on that kind of case, but it pays the bills."

"Yes, there's a lot of adultery going on," grinned Halliday, who had never been tempted in that direction. His wife made sure of that.

"It's Pearl, actually. Well, and Dilys too, of course."

"Are you going through with the divorce, then?"

"I want to but it's all such a filthy business. I don't see why I should be the one to provide the evidence when it's Pearl who wanted to go off with Dean."

"Yes, I know. But you fancied Dilys at the same time. And she's a married woman."

"Okay, okay. I hold my hands up. But her husband is happy to give her a divorce, while Pearl's making it very difficult for me."

"She still wants to try and make a go of it, then?"

Barney shrugged. "I suppose so."

"And you don't?"

"No. I know I should, but I don't love her anymore. I'm not sure I ever did. I married her too soon after – after Marianne. I wasn't thinking straight. It's Dilys I love."

"Tricky," observed Halliday.

"Anyway, enough of my troubles. How about you? Got any interesting cases going on? Any juicy murders?"

"I wondered when you would ask," grinned the Inspector. "I've just got stuck with this case. I must have 'muggins' stamped on my forehead or something. No one else wanted to handle it."

"Really? Why's that?"

"A charlady's been murdered."

"A charlady? Who would want to murder a charlady?"

"A charlady is just as likely to be a murder victim as anyone else, I suppose," said Halliday with a sigh. "It does seem a bit bizarre, though. And there's no obvious motive, either."

"What happened to her, then?"

"She was found drowned in her own mop bucket on the third floor of the offices of a finance firm in Cannon Street."

"Has it been reported in the papers? I don't recall seeing anything about it."

"There was a bit about it in a couple of the red tops. That's all. Not really sexy enough to grab the headlines. If she had been a glamorous blonde, they'd have gone to town. Poor woman."

"Could it have been suicide?"

"No, that's been ruled out by the pathologist. He said there was a contusion – they love saying that word, pathologists – a bruise, whatever, on the side of her head. It means she was hit over the nut before being drowned in her bucket."

"Nasty," said Barney, showing a flicker of interest at last.

"Yes, as you say, 'nasty'. The woman seemed a perfectly respectable individual with a husband and grown-up daughter. They don't have any idea why anyone should want to kill her."

"Bit of a puzzle for you, then?"

"You could say that."

Halliday sighed and stared through the window at the people seated outside the pub enjoying the sunshine. He wished he could enjoy it too, but this charwoman business was weighing heavily on him. And Barney, in his present mood, was no help. He supposed he hadn't expected anything, really. After all, there seemed no motive for the murder and therefore no obvious suspect.

"Better be making tracks, old chap," said Halliday now, standing up. Barney stood too and they shook hands. "If you come up with any ideas, well – you know."

"Of course, Tony. Will do."

But Halliday could already see that Barney hadn't taken in his request. He couldn't blame him, he supposed.

He continued to puzzle over his murder case as he made his way to the tube station. Then his thoughts wandered to poor Barney. Women! he thought with exasperation. Whether they were being murdered or just being plain difficult, they were a bloody nuisance most of the time.

3

Daisy Carmichael looked lovingly at her little son, Michael. Then she looked far less lovingly at Pearl Carmichael, who had dropped in uninvited for 'tea and a chat'.

"I think he should sleep for a couple of hours now," said Daisy, making sure Michael wasn't too hot in his cot. The sun was streaming in through the nursery window as she and Pearl stood looking at the snuffling two-year-old.

"Good as gold," observed Pearl, smiling.

"Well, let's go downstairs and I'll put the kettle on," said Daisy at last. Her precious son was in the Land of Nod and all was right with the world. Almost. There was, of course, Pearl.

"I've got either custard creams or some jam sponge from yesterday," said Daisy, rummaging in the larder. "Can't guarantee how fresh it is."

"Custard creams will be fine."

They were seated in the kitchen which had recently undergone a facelift. Daisy was proud of the new, up-to-the-minute units on the walls and under the sink, as well as the new fully automatic washing machine which had replaced the old, unreliable twin tub. There were lots of new gadgets too, including a brand new food mixer. She was gratified to see the envious look in Pearl's eyes as she looked around.

"So, Pearl, how are things?" Daisy didn't care, but felt obliged to make conversation. As far as she was concerned, Barney's erring wife could go and take a running jump. Poor Barney didn't deserve such a selfish woman.

Daisy knew all about the difficulties her brother-in-law was going through trying to get a divorce. Pearl knew which side her bread was buttered, apparently. She had been fully prepared to leave Barney for Dean Bannister, her partner in their acrobatic act. However, Dean had thought better of it and now had a new girlfriend. This new girlfriend was also partnering him in the acrobatic act, which had left Pearl precisely nowhere. It was no wonder she wanted to cling on to Barney. He was like a life raft in a stormy sea.

"Oh, you know," said Pearl, sipping her tea slowly. She bit into a custard cream.

"I don't, actually," said Daisy, "otherwise I wouldn't have wasted my breath asking." The obvious animosity in her words and manner seemed to have no effect on Pearl, however.

"Well, I'm going in with this new acrobatic act, which is one good thing, at least."

"New acrobatic act?"

"Yes. I've just signed a contract. Two men and a girl. We're called 'High Jinks'."

Daisy smirked. "Funny name."

"Well, it's because we'll be doing lots of high wire stuff. I'm a bit out of practice with the trapeze but I'm getting back into it."

"So, how did you find this act?"

"They were already established, but the girl they had got herself pregnant, so they had to find someone else. My agent put me in touch."

"I wish you luck. When do you start?"

"We've got our first booking in Manchester in about three weeks. Meantime, we're rehearsing like mad. They think I'm fitting in well."

"That's good." Daisy finished her tea, secretly wishing Pearl would get to the point. She had dropped in for a reason, she was sure. Or maybe she had come to tell her about the new act, although she wasn't sure why Pearl would have thought she'd be that interested. There had been no love lost between the two women almost right from the start. But since Daisy had found out about Pearl's betrayal, their relationship had gone steadily downhill.

"The real reason I came to see you is …." Pearl trailed off. The look on Daisy's face gave nothing away.

Both women sat in silence in the sunny kitchen. It would have been pleasant if the two women had been friends but, as it was, the scent of Jim's prize roses wafting through the open back door went completely unnoticed.

"Come on, Pearl. I'm listening." Daisy said at last. The sooner she said what she came to say, the sooner she'd leave.

"I wondered if you'd – you'd put in a good word for me."

"What? A sort of reference, do you mean? For your new job? Surely you don't need to provide references for that line of work?"

"You're deliberately misunderstanding me," said Pearl, a note of bitterness in her voice.

Daisy didn't reply. Instead, she ate the last custard cream on the plate.

"You could talk to Jim. Say how unhappy I am and how much I want Barney to – well, to think better of me, at least. I made a mistake. I thought I was in love with Dean. I know now it's always been Barney."

"When you knew you couldn't have Dean."

Pearl sighed and stood up, brushing biscuit crumbs from her skirt. "I see there's no point in talking to you."

Daisy shrugged. She rose to show her out. "I don't know why I should help you. You broke Barney's heart."

Pearl turned on her. "I don't think so, Daisy. He's not so upset as all that. He's got someone else, hasn't he? That's why he wants a divorce."

Daisy felt sorry for her now. There was truth in what she had just said. It took two to tango and all that. Barney wasn't completely blameless for the failure of their marriage.

"All right, Pearl. I'll talk to Jim. See if there's anything he can do. I don't hold out much hope, though."

"Th-thanks, anyway," said Pearl, giving her a weak smile as they air-kissed goodbye.

Daisy closed the door on her sister-in-law with a sigh. She could hear her son begin to whimper. Smiling to herself, she climbed the stairs to the nursery. Poor Pearl. She'd bet she was more than a little jealous of her being a mother. That would solve everything if she got pregnant. Barney wouldn't leave her then.

Her hand went involuntarily to her stomach, resting on it protectively as she looked in the cot at her fractious little boy. She picked him up and felt the warmth of his little body as she held him close.

4

Jim Carmichael sometimes missed the stage. He had been a juggler and trick cyclist in an act with brother Barney for many years until both men reached their dodgy forties and Barney decided he wanted to be Humphrey Bogart. To be fair to his brother, Jim knew he hadn't taken the decision lightly. His nerve was going and his balance was going with it. So, he had decided to quit before a major accident occurred.

The private investigation agency was Barney's solution. It was also what he had wanted to do all his life. It was just a pity it wasn't what Jim wanted as well. He would have liked to carry on with the act a little longer, but it wasn't only impossible because of Barney's defection. Pearl and Dean had managed to ease him out, taking the act over and making it their own as they did so. There was no room, it seemed, for a middle-aged man, even if his circus skills were just as good as theirs.

Jim had taken the disappointment well, weaning himself off 'the smell of the greasepaint and roar of the crowd' gradually. Barney, meanwhile, had enlisted his services just as gradually, until Jim was at last a fully-fledged member of the detective agency team. 'Team' was a bit of an exaggeration, as it only consisted of the two of them. Pearl had helped occasionally but since falling out with her husband, she stayed away.

Muriel Bird, Jim could tell at once, was going to be a great asset to the 'team' and it wasn't just because she had a nice pair of legs. She smiled at him as he entered the office. It was her third morning, and, to Jim, she looked just right sitting at her typewriter. Barney was out on a missing husband case following a dead end, as he firmly believed. He boiled the kettle for coffee and placed a mug on her desk.

"Ooh, thanks," she said. "Shouldn't it be me making it for you?"

Jim smiled and shrugged as he sipped his brew. "No problem," he said. "You can make me one later. How are you settling in?"

Muriel, who was dressed in a light summer frock that showed off all her feminine assets, wriggled in her chair and crossed her slender legs with a provocative motion. At least it seemed provocative to Jim, who had led a fairly sheltered life. He liked what he saw.

"Fine, fine," she said. "I was hoping it would be a bit more interesting, though. Do we just deal in missing cats?"

"Oh, no, not only cats," grinned Jim, "sometimes dogs, as well."

She laughed. "No, seriously," she said, "don't you ever get mysterious clients turn up with unusual problems like in *The Maltese Falcon*?"

"Oh, you mean a beautiful, mysterious woman comes into a rundown private dick's office and asks for his help in finding her sister who's been kidnapped by a vicious gang because she knows something she shouldn't? That kind of thing?"

"Well, no, not quite. I know you get these boring missing husband cases – a lot of that. Divorce stuff. But I thought there might be the occasional something different."

"Well, we've had our moments," said Jim, remembering. "In fact, Barney nearly got himself killed a couple of times."

Muriel's large hazel eyes grew even wider at this. "Gosh!" she said. "You wouldn't think it to look at him."

"Well, he's all right, now," laughed Jim, "but I know what you mean. With that baby face of his, he doesn't quite fit the hero-type."

"I didn't mean that, exactly," said Muriel. "Just that, well, I've only seen him writing reports and going out to find missing cats and things."

"You've only been here a couple of days, Muriel," said Jim, finishing his coffee. "You'll see some action soon, I expect."

She gave a little cough. "Er …" she began.

"Yes?" Jim was beginning to like her more and more. He hoped this like wasn't going to develop into anything more dangerous. After all, she was a married woman, and his own marriage was precious to him. Besides, she was young enough to be his daughter.

"I was wondering if – at some stage …." She trailed off again.

"Spit it out."

"If – well, if I might be allowed to do some actual investigating myself?"

"You?" Jim was taken aback. This pretty young thing? Getting into danger? It was all very well for him and Barney. They were blokes. But this slip of a girl? No, not possibly.

"Yes."

"We couldn't possibly allow you to get into any danger," he said in what he hoped wasn't a too avuncular manner. He didn't want to appear a fuddy-duddy in her eyes, although he supposed it was inevitable, given the difference in their ages.

"I don't want to be a secretary all my life," she muttered, obviously upset with him. "I want some excitement before I settle down to babies and washing nappies."

Jim felt sorry for her. Women didn't have a great time, he supposed. While men could get away from such mundane tasks by going to work, once a woman had a baby it was her lot to stay at home. He thought of Daisy. But she was happy to be at home with Michael, she had assured him constantly. Although, just recently, she seemed a bit restless. Moody, even. He supposed he'd have to find out what was wrong sooner or later, but he hated any kind of confrontation. He loved his wife very much but sometimes she could be a bit of a nag.

"Well, look," he said, trying not to stare at Muriel's shapely legs. His eyes travelled upwards, but then realized he was looking at her breasts. That was even worse. "Er, you must be patient. Once you have been here a while, maybe – I mean, I'd have to see what Barney says."

"Okay, thanks." She didn't look happy with Jim's answer. Jim was upset too. If she began to make a nuisance of herself, perhaps she was wrong for them after all. They only wanted a secretary, not Danger Woman.

There was now an uneasy atmosphere as Muriel continued typing and Jim returned to his accounts ledger. The balance was in the black, which was good. More money was coming in than was going out. He tried to concentrate on this, but every so often he stole a glance at the girl, her head bent over her work as her fingers flew over the keys. She was a good typist, he thought. Why couldn't she be content with that? He didn't know what her husband did for a living, but he reckoned he was probably bringing in a good wage. Soon she would get pregnant and that would sort out the immediate problem. He hoped so, anyway. He turned over a page in the ledger.

5

Barney returned to the office later that afternoon in a bad mood. As Jim had predicted, he had been on a wild goose chase. Jim smiled and was about to say that he had told him so, but saw the look on his brother's face just in time.

"No luck, then?" he said unnecessarily.

"Not so's you'd notice it." Barney slumped behind his desk and glared at Jim. "Where's Muriel?"

"She's gone home," Jim replied, looking at the clock. "It's gone half-past five and she's her husband's tea to get."

"Is it as late as that?"

"You must have been enjoying yourself, not noticing the time."

"Ha bloody ha."

"Sorry, old man. Just a little joke."

"Just a little one," Barney agreed.

"Anyway, you can put in a hefty bill for expenses to cover your wasted time," Jim pointed out. He switched on the kettle as he said this. "Coffee? Tea?"

"Any whisky?"

"That bad, eh?"

"I sometimes wonder what we're doing, Jim." Barney's face was grey with exhaustion. He undid his collar and rubbed his fingers inside. His neck was bathed in sweat.

"This stifling heat doesn't help," he sighed.

"Look, why don't we close up and go for a drink? A long cool lager? Sound good?"

"Sounds very good but I need to write up my report for the client, before I forget what I did exactly. Then there's my expenses to work out. I intend to squeeze every penny out of this one."

"Okay, as you like. I think I'll go now, though, if that's all right with you?"

"It's fine. Is that for me?" Barney took the cup of steaming tea from Jim. "Thanks." He took a sip. "Can I pop round later?"

"Sure," said Jim.

After Jim had gone, Barney sat staring at the wall for several minutes. He removed his tie altogether and draped it over the arm of his chair. He rubbed his neck once more. It felt red raw and he realized he was dog-tired. It wasn't the first time he felt despair at the career path he had chosen for himself. Following unfaithful husbands into seedy hotels wasn't what he had intended when he first set up the agency. True, he had had some interesting, not to say dangerous, cases, but they were few and far between. His days were mostly spent sitting outside people's houses, watching for any suspicious movements. Night as well as day. He wasn't getting a lot of sleep.

His domestic life wasn't much better either. He hadn't seen Dilys lately. She had kept her distance once she knew Pearl was making difficulties.

"I won't be the reason for the breakup of your marriage," she had told him.

Barney had come close to strangling Pearl, even if it was only in his head. But when it came down to it, she was still his wife. Dilys was someone else's. It made no difference that Dilys's husband was in the process of leaving her, as Pearl wasn't prepared to divorce Barney and Barney had no choice but to accept it.

He sipped the hot tea. It passed through his mind that it was the last thing he needed on a day like this. But it was Indian tea and Indians drank tea all the time even though their climate was hardly arctic. He'd once read somewhere that drinking hot tea was the best thing in a heat wave. It was something to do with how it made you sweat which helped to cool you down. Those Indians were a canny lot. They knew a thing or two, an ancient culture like theirs.

All this irrelevant stuff whirled around his brain as he continued to sip the tea and sweat even more as he did so. Then, suddenly, he actually began to cool down. It works! he thought, trying to concentrate on his report. He wanted to get it written out so that it would be ready for Muriel to type in the morning.

They'd made a good choice, choosing her. But, though she certainly brightened up the place, there was something about her that unsettled him slightly. He couldn't put his finger on it, but maybe Jim felt the same too. It was probably just a period of adjustment. Two blokes and a girl could be a tricky scenario if you weren't used to it. Maybe he'd mention it to Jim when he went round there later.

He often liked to look in on his brother and sister-in-law in the evenings, appreciating the happy family atmosphere so different from what he could expect when he got home to Pearl. Even though she rarely had his supper ready for him, she would still would find a reason to nag him for being late. If it was Dilys he was going home to, he would have been there by now. Dilys was the love of his life but Pearl stood in the way. Why couldn't his wife see that staying together was making them both unhappy? If she could accept that, she'd soon find someone more her own age. There'd be any number of offers, a looker like Pearl.

He shook himself out of his reverie and continued to write up his report. It wasn't a long one, as it basically consisted of: *followed 'A' from 9 am until 5 pm. Nothing out of the ordinary to report*. But he had to stretch it out a bit, if only to justify the expenses he intended to charge. Barney had never been gifted with a vivid imagination so it was proving rather difficult.

6

Barney sighed with relief as he finished the report at last. He doubted his client would be very happy with it as it told her precisely nothing. On the other hand, she should be pleased he hadn't found any evidence her husband was having an illicit affair. Barney was the one who was unhappy, being faced with another boring day following the man around, his camera at the ready to take any compromising photos. Chance would be a fine thing, he thought as he put the scribbled pages on Muriel's desk. He wrote an instruction to her: 'one copy and two carbons'. Then he remembered to add 'please' and 'thanks'.

He put on his tie, preparing to leave the office. He hoped it had cooled down a bit outside. Looking out of the window, he watched the passers-by in their skimpy clothes: men in their shirt sleeves (rolled up, he noted with disgust) and women in dresses that left little to the imagination, even Barney's limited one.

Then it happened. The moment he had been waiting for it seemed like forever, although it was more probably from the moment he set up the detective agency. There was a small tap on the door and, before he could ask who it was at this time of the evening, a woman entered. Her scent overpowered him at first, then he saw her properly. She was Mary Astor in *The Maltese Falcon*, here to consult Barney 'Humphrey Bogart' Carmichael.

He took in her appearance, hardly believing his eyes. Her hair was immaculately permanently waved, blonde and glistening, and her eyes, which he thought were probably very beautiful, were hidden behind sunglasses. Her stiletto heels click-clacked across the floor towards him. As it was too hot, the furs she would inevitably be draped in were absent, but Barney had no doubt she had them. Today, however, she was wearing a lace shawl across her elegant shoulders, and her streamlined linen dress had no creases in it. It didn't dare. This woman was not to be trifled with.

"Hello, young man," said the woman in a soft but unmistakable New York accent. It was almost too much for poor Barney. "Have I the pleasure of addressing Mr Barney Carmichael of Carmichael Private Investigation Services?"

"Yes, madam," said Barney deferentially. "That's me."

Without waiting to be asked, she sat in the chair in front of Barney's desk and crossed her legs with an elegant and refined movement.

He hadn't the faintest idea where to find the Maltese Falcon, but he'd do his damnedest to try. After all, he was quite good at finding parrots, so a falcon shouldn't be that much of a problem. Although a gold model of one might be more difficult, he supposed. Then he pulled himself together as she continued to speak.

"My name is Jeanne Conrad, Mrs Jeanne Conrad."

"How d'you do?"

"I'll come straight to the point, Mr Carmichael. I want you to find my son."

"Find your son?" Barney echoed.

"Here is a recent picture of him." She passed a photograph across the desk to him.

Barney looked at a well set up young man in his mid-twenties. Fair hair and an engaging smile. He wore a polo neck sweater and was holding a dog of some description. The breed escaped him.

So, this woman must be in her forties, at least, Barney reckoned. Maybe if he could see her eyes, he'd be able to estimate her age more correctly, but the sunglasses remained in place. He refrained from telling her she hardly looked old enough to have such a grown-up son. She didn't look the type for flattery. However, she did look the type to pay well.

"Er, can I ask – do you live in London?"

"No, I'm just on a visit." She removed a gold cigarette case from her handbag and opened it. She leaned forward and offered it to him. The cigarettes were long and slim. Elegant, like herself.

"Er, no thanks, I'm trying to give them up." Barney knew that his god Bogart would have accepted one, but then he didn't know how bad they were for you back then, even though he had probably died as the result of smoking them.

She snapped the case shut and proceeded to insert a cigarette into a holder. She put it in her mouth and waited for Barney to light it. He fumbled in his desk drawer for the lighter he only used occasionally now, mainly for clients. His hand trembled as he did the honours.

"Thanks," she said, blowing smoke into his face. He tried not to cough.

Barney picked up the photo of the woman's son and stared at it intently. "So, is your son here – in London?" He had visions of having to fly to the States, something he'd always wanted to do, but could never afford to. But if this woman had the wherewithal to finance such a trip …

She was speaking. "So I understand."

"London's a big place," said Barney, hiding his disappointment as the Statue of Liberty receded from his mind. "Have you any idea where exactly your son could have gone?"

"I have an address," she said and passed him a piece of paper.

44 Cairo Road, Stockwell. He put the photo and the address into his wallet which was in his jacket pocket hanging over the back of his chair. "Thanks, that should help," he said. "What's your son's name, by the way?"

"Leon – Leon Conrad. Please find him for me, young man."

Barney, who was far from being a young man although his baby face made him look like one, gave her a reassuring smile. "I'll do my best. Here are our terms and conditions." He took a typewritten sheet from the pile in one of the overflowing trays on his desk and passed it to her.

She waved an expertly manicured hand in the air. "I don't need to see those. I just want you to find my son. Money is no object. Whatever it takes." She rose. "I'm staying at Claridges. You can reach me on this number." She took a gold-embossed card out of her bag and handed it to Barney. "That's the hotel switchboard. Ask for room 321. I've written it there."

Barney studied the card before putting it in his wallet along with the photo of Leon Conrad and the address where he was to start looking for him.

"Thank you. Er, may I ask – what is the significance of Cairo Road?"

"That's no concern of yours," she said stiffly. "Just find my son. Call me when you have and leave the rest to me."

A few minutes later, the office was back to normal. It was as if the last few minutes had never happened. If it hadn't been for the lingering smell of her perfume, Barney would have assumed he'd dreamed the whole thing.

As if to reassure himself that it had really happened, he looked again at the photograph of the smiling Leon Conrad. He wondered if he wanted to be found and quickly came to the conclusion that he probably didn't. Otherwise, why not tell his mother where he was going? Still, that wasn't Barney's problem. All he had to do was go to 44 Cairo Road and check that he was there.

But if that were the case, he suddenly thought, then why didn't Mrs Conrad go there herself?

He locked up the office and walked to the lift, pondering this mystery. He thought, with gratification, that this was what his real work was all about. It was what he had gone into this business for. Humphrey Bogart wouldn't shirk from this assignment, and neither would Barney Carmichael, even if it did lead him into a web of intrigue and danger.

He pressed the ground floor button. The lift jerked him to the street and the heat hit him as he walked to his car. He realised he was feeling happier than he had for months.

7

Jim had been wanting a cold beer all day. He stood outside the pub, hands in pockets, shirt sleeves rolled up. He had told Barney he was stopping off for a beer and had invited him to join him. He had refused, pleading pressure of work, making him wonder if his brother didn't entirely approve. That was Barney all over. He couldn't understand how Jim could put off going home to his wife and little boy. He was envious of their happy marriage, and it was a happy marriage. Most of the time.

Jim loved Daisy just as much as ever he did, even though familiarity with a woman he had courted for twelve years before marrying her just over three years ago could have bred the contempt the proverb tells us it does. But Jim, far from contempt, had the utmost love and respect for his wife. He had thoughts about other women, naturally. He wouldn't be human if he didn't. But his thoughts never extended into any kind of reality.

The close proximity of a pretty girl was something he was able to cope with, he told himself. Muriel Bird was a pretty girl, but she was just that. He stopped right there.

He continued to hesitate in front of the pub door. Perhaps he should go straight home, after all? The stifling heat was winning, however, and before he could think any further, he was inside.

It was just what he needed. He drank his pint in two goes and wiped the froth from his lips with satisfaction. He looked towards the back of the pub and saw that the doors were thrown open onto the garden where he could see lots of people sitting, enjoying a smoke and drink at the end of the summer day. It was a pleasing sight. He felt strongly tempted to buy another pint and join them, but resisted. He must get home to Daisy.

But she was so edgy these days and didn't seem very well. He had heard her vomiting only the other morning but she hadn't said anything so he had decided not to say anything either. He hoped she wasn't going to be ill. If so, he wouldn't be able to cope with his two-year-old and hold down the job. It was probably just something she'd eaten. Yes, that was it. Something she'd eaten. Come to think of it, those prawns they'd had the other night could have been fresher. He hadn't suffered any ill effects, but then he had a cast iron stomach.

Daisy greeted him with her usual peck on the cheek and seemed a bit brighter than when he had left her that morning. He perked up immediately.

"Only salad, I'm afraid," she told him. "Couldn't be bothered to cook in this heat."

"Salad'll do me fine," he said, meaning it. She was right. It was much too hot for stew and dumplings. "How was your day?"

"Oh, the usual," she shrugged.

They were seated at the dining table that looked out over the back garden. It was a pleasant view. However, the open window was encouraging gnats, bees and wasps to hover over the tomatoes and radishes. Jim picked out the food carefully, brushing aside a particularly obstinate wasp. He'd always thought they preferred sweet things like jam to rabbit food.

"Me too." He bit into the crisp lettuce and found it surprisingly tasty.

"Oh, by the way, I had a visitor," said Daisy suddenly.

"Oh. Who was that?"

"Pearl."

He stared at her. "Pearl?"

"Yes, Pearl."

"What did she want?"

"She wanted me to have a word with you about Barney. She thinks you'll be able to persuade him to stay with her. Not sure why she thinks that, though."

"Neither do I. I don't know what she thinks I can do. As far as I can tell, their marriage is over. And I've no intention of interfering. It's Barney's life."

"It's not that simple."

"Nothing ever is."

It was a brief, staccato conversation, ending with Daisy removing the dishes in meaningful silence.

Jim retired to the front room with the newspaper. After all, what else was there to say? Barney didn't love Pearl. He didn't trust her. And he loved someone else. That was that.

"I'm just going to check on Michael and then I want to watch the telly," Daisy called from the kitchen.

He glanced at the clock. Oh yes, he sighed to himself. Nearly half-past seven on a Wednesday. Bloody *Coronation Street*. What she saw in the goings on of Elsie Tanner and Ena Sharples, he couldn't fathom.

He could hear the almost funereal *Coronation Street* theme, telling him the programme was over when the doorbell rang. Barney looked very excited as he followed Jim through the house towards the back garden. Daisy greeted him as they passed and carried on watching the television. A noisy game show was now in progress. If the two men had been more observant, they would have noticed her knitting or, more precisely, *what* she was knitting.

"So, what's up?" laughed Jim as he handed his brother a cold can of lager from the fridge.

"It's happened at last," he replied, an enigmatic smile on his round face.

"What has?"

"The dream job."

"Dream job?" Jim knew Barney had always seen himself as Philip Marlowe, but that was just a fantasy. Lauren Bacall was never going to come into the office and ask him if he knew how to whistle.

"Yes. A woman. A mysterious woman."

Or was she? "Mysterious? How so?"

Barney proceeded to tell Jim all about the visit of Mrs Conrad. He embellished it here and there, but in all essentials, it was like something out of the pages of Dashiell Hammett.

"Wow!" was all Jim could think of to say.

"Interesting, eh?"

"Yes, it certainly would seem so. But, I mean, why doesn't she just go to this Cairo Road address herself, if she knows her son is there?"

"My thoughts exactly. I can't wait to get started. I'll go round there first thing tomorrow."

Jim looked doubtful. "All right, Barney. But – "

"But what?" Barney finished his lager and squashed the can.

Jim did the same. "Be careful. That's all."

Barney gave him a look, but said nothing.

Jim patted him on the shoulder. "I'm sure it'll be fine. But – well – you could be walking into some sort of a trap."

Barney laughed. "Oh, for goodness sake, Jim. This is London, England, nineteen-sixty-one. Not nineteen-twenties Chicago. What on earth could happen? I'm just going to knock on a door in a suburban London street."

"It's what's behind the door that worries me," said Jim. He hoped his brother wasn't going to be duffed up again. Or worse.

8

Barney found Cairo Road in Stockwell after he had driven past it three times. To be fair, it was an insignificant little road, easily missed if one had never been there before.

Parking his car at the bottom of it, he got out and surveyed the prospect with some dismay. It wasn't the most picturesque of roads and most of the houses looked run down and neglected. And even though the sun was shining as brightly as ever, it seemed to be making little impression on the overall shadowy darkness of the road itself. There were several properties with 'for sale' signs outside, and one or two looked like they'd been there for years. No wonder, he thought. Who'd want to live down a street like this?

However, it was suitably dark and mysterious, appropriate for private detective work. Barney felt a shiver go up his spine as he walked along, despite the heat of the day.

He passed house after house, looking for number 44. That's funny, he thought. There's number 42 and there's number 46 but there's no number 44. It should be between them, surely? What was going on?

He crossed over to the odd-numbered side. Every number was an odd one, as he expected, so number 44 wasn't to be found there either. It was now very hot; the early morning cool having evaporated before it had even begun. Barney wasn't one to undress in public, but he was sorely tempted to remove his coat and tie. He resisted the temptation, however, and walked up the path of number 46 Cairo Road instead.

His ring was answered almost immediately by an elderly woman in garish pink carpet slippers and a dress of nondescript hue which seemed to hang on her as if she was a coat hanger. Her complexion was almost the same tint as her dress. In fact, the carpet slippers were the only splash of colour on her entire person, her eyes being almost white with cataracts.

Barney raised his hat politely. "Hello," he said, giving her a cheery smile. "I'm sorry to bother you, but I'm looking for number 44. I can't seem to find it."

"Well, you won't, young man," came the reply.

"Oh?"

"It was changed some time ago," she continued. "Number 44 is now number 42."

"Er, I see." He didn't see at all. The hot sun was bothering him still more now. His skin felt itchy and the desire to scratch was almost unbearable.

"All the houses were renumbered up until mine, starting off with number 2 and 2A. Some of the residents objected at the time, but most of them have long gone now."

"There does seem to be a lot of houses for sale down this road," Barney observed. He was praying she would invite him in for a cold drink, but it didn't look promising. He persisted, however.

"Have you been living here a long time yourself?"

"What's it to you?"

The old woman's sudden rudeness threw him slightly. Then he regained his confidence.

"I'm a private investigator – I'm – "

"Oh, why didn't you say?" she said with enthusiasm. "Come in, young man, come in."

"Perhaps you'd better see my card first?" Barney showed her his card as she more or less pushed him into the hall which was even darker than the shadowy street outside. The fanlight at the top of the front door was doing its best to let in a shaft of sunlight, but failing miserably.

She gazed at the wording without seeing it. "That's all right," she said, ushering him into a small parlour that smelt of lavender polish and cats. There were two felines discernible on the window ledge and Barney could feel another one insinuate itself around his legs.

"Would you like a cup of tea?" she asked, shooing the cat away.

Barney would have preferred a cold drink and a clothes brush. The cat's black hairs were clearly visible on his light grey summer trousers.

"Er, thank you, but do you have a glass of water instead?"

"Water?" She was looking at him as if he was mad. "In the tap."

"Would it – would it be too much trouble to bring me a glass?" He was beginning to feel faint.

She trundled off to the kitchen, muttering. Barney, meanwhile, wiped his sweating brow and watched the two window-sitting cats with fascination. He liked cats as a general rule, when he didn't have to find missing ones, of course. These two (one ginger, the other tortoiseshell) were obviously content and well-fed, and therefore unlikely to go missing. If he knew anything at all about cats, they knew where they were well off.

The old lady was back with the water. He took it gratefully and gulped it down. It was warm, but welcome nonetheless.

"Now," she said, seating herself in the fireside chair, indicating the sofa for him. "How can I help? Are you on the trail of a murderer or international drug smuggler?"

"Er, no," he laughed. "Nothing quite like that." At least he didn't think so, but you never knew your luck. "I'm trying to find a missing son. The last known address I was given by his mother was 44 Cairo Road. Which appears to be missing too."

She laughed. "The police gave up on that over twenty years ago. You've got no chance of finding him now. Have you got a picture of this missing son?"

"Yes, here." He handed her the photo of the young man with the disarming smile and, now he came to look at it again, a smattering of freckles over his well-shaped nose.

"Why, this young man was here just over a week ago."

"Here? You mean you saw him? Spoke to him?"

"Yes, I certainly did." She paused, as if for effect. "You see, he told me he was looking for his mother."

9

"I don't know what to think."

Barney made this statement to brother Jim that evening as they sat in the crowded garden attached to the Fox and Hounds public house. His visit to Cairo Road, far from clearing up the mystery of the missing son, had only served to deepen it. The most likely explanation was Mrs Ridley was mistaken. The young man who had visited her probably resembled Leon Conrad. Yes, that was it, he reasoned. And her eyesight didn't look that good. The way she had peered at Leon's photo through her unnaturally pale eyes told him that.

Jim fished in his trouser pocket for his hankie and mopped the sweat from his brow with it.

"Phew! This heat is really too much. They said on the radio this morning that Spain was cooler than here."

"Have you been listening to what I've been saying?" Barney's tone was irritable with the heat and the frustration of his assignment.

"Yes, of course. I don't know what to think either," was Jim's unhelpful reply.

"And what do you make of the missing 44? Why would they have renumbered the houses like that?"

Jim looked thoughtful. He leaned his elbows on the iron table which made it wobble dangerously.

"Careful!" admonished Barney. "You're spilling my drink."

"Sorry. Look, this number business. You say they renumbered from 2, making the next one 2A and so all the houses would have changed numbers up until 44, which now doesn't exist? Number 46, who you visited, would still be as it was. I think that's right?"

Barney thought for a moment. "Yes, I agree. That would be right."

"Therefore, logically, the new number 42 would be the old number 44. I mean they never demolished it, did they? Whoever 'they' were."

"Exactly."

"So, the house you should have visited would have been number 42, not number 46." Jim looked triumphant.

"Of course. I'm not daft. I couldn't go there for the simple reason that it's unoccupied. There's a 'for sale' sign up and the place looks as though it's been deserted for years."

"Hmm, I see." Jim's triumphant expression slowly disappeared. "That makes it more difficult."

"But what I want to know is – why on earth did they renumber the houses in the first place? It doesn't make any sense."

Jim's look of triumph returned. "The answer's simple. Something horrible must have happened there, something so awful that the neighbourhood wanted to obliterate it. Think of Rillington Place. They renamed that, didn't they? Or, no. They demolished the street altogether, I think."

Barney looked shocked. "You don't mean there could have been some gruesome murders in that house?" The heinous crimes of John Reginald Halliday Christie were still vivid in the minds of most people, a mere ten years or so after they had been committed.

"No, I'm not saying that. But something must have happened there, all the same. Otherwise, why would they renumber the houses? I mean, they'd never be able to sell a house if some awful crime had been committed in it, would they? At least, not easily."

Barney finished his pint quickly. The wobbly table was threatening to spill it again as Jim stretched his long legs under it. "You've given me an idea," he said. "The newspaper archives. I could search there. See if I can find reports of any crimes in 44 Cairo Road."

"Tall order," observed Jim. "I mean, where would you start? What year, for example?"

Barney looked dashed now. "Someone must know something," he said. "I'll go back tomorrow and try a few more doors. I'll also revisit old Mrs Ridley, because I bet she knows more than she's letting on."

"Okay, Barney. That sounds like a good idea. Another pint?" He still had to do Daisy's bidding and speak to his brother about Pearl.

Both men were reluctant to return home, and both men knew each other's reasons without having to spell them out. Although Barney was only vaguely aware of Daisy's moods, Jim, of course, knew only too well the kind of life Pearl was leading his brother. He had told him about Pearl's visit to Daisy and the reason for it. Barney's reaction had been exactly as he expected. He wasn't in the least interested in trying to make a go of his marriage, and Jim didn't try to change his mind.

So, they both sat on in the hot pub garden with refreshed drinks, as the sun began to loosen its grip. Twilight was approaching, lights were twinkling, and shadows were spreading comfortingly across the grass. Many after-work drinkers had departed, so Barney and Jim had the place almost to themselves, apart from one family with several noisy and fidgety children. One child had spilt his lemonade and was screaming at his poor mother who, looking decidedly hot and cross, was dabbing at his tee shirt in an attempt to mop up the worst of the fizzy spillage.

"How – how's Daisy these days?" Barney ventured to ask after a few moments' friendly silence. The crickets chirped happily in that silence, and somewhere a robin or some such London bird made a 'getting his family ready for bed' sort of noise. It was pleasant, more pleasant, thought both men, than being at home at that moment.

"Oh, she's fine," said Jim, unconvincingly.

"She – she still a bit fed up with you?"

"Don't know what the problem is. She just seems depressed or worried. But whenever I ask her what's wrong, she says it's nothing and I shouldn't fuss."

"Has she recovered from her sickness now? Food poisoning, wasn't it?"

"That's just it. She was sick again this morning."

"Oh dear. Perhaps she should see a doctor."

"I told her she should, but she just ignored me."

"I bet I know what's wrong," said Barney suddenly.

"You do?"

"Have you thought she might be pregnant?"

Jim was thunderstruck. His hand shook as he raised his glass to his lips. The thought had crossed his mind too, but he had dismissed it almost at once. Several times.

"No, she can't be," he said. The tone of his voice was sombre.

"Oh, I'm sorry. Can't she have any more children, then?"

"It's not that. You see – "

"What?"

"The doctor told us after Michael was born, to have any more kids could be dangerous. For her. You see, she had a really bad time with Michael and, I never told you this – "

"What, Jim? What is it?"

"She nearly died."

10

The night was still young as far as Barney was concerned. Jim had hurried away after dropping his bombshell. He would no doubt be home now, he thought, finding out what he feared was true. Why hadn't his brother confided in him before? Maybe he thought the matter would never arise, so why bother him with something he could do nothing about.

Barney couldn't bear the thought of a bereaved brother. Purely selfish in his outlook at that moment, all he needed was a miserable Jim while Pearl was being so difficult. Jim was his rock, he couldn't bear the thought of him crumbling away.

He continued to sit on in the pub garden, twilight now almost full-blown night. The family with the annoying children had gone and there was only one other couple still sitting there. The smoke from their cigarettes filled the air. Barney felt like lighting up himself, but resisted the temptation. He already had an irritating cough in the mornings, and the bout of bronchitis he had suffered in January had frightened him. Dilys had scolded him and instructed him to give up the nicotine forthwith. He had more or less done so, apart from the occasional slip.

Now, tonight, he wanted to see Dilys more than ever. Her husband had left her, so he knew she would be on her own. He had tried not to contact her, but tonight the urge to hold her in his arms was too strong. Either that, or he'd have to smoke a cigarette.

Dilys wouldn't welcome him, even if he took a chance and went to see her. She had made it quite clear that, while Pearl was still his wife, she wouldn't have anything to do with him. She had even hinted that her husband wanted to come back and she was considering it, but Barney didn't believe her. She had only said that to keep him at arm's length, he was sure.

He left the pub garden through the back gate and, despite his resolve not to visit her, he found himself half-an-hour later outside Dilys's house in Finchley. He pulled up and braked noisily. Three pints of beer had something to do with his awkward parking, but he didn't acknowledge it. He could hold his drink all right. It was just that the pavement edge was uneven. It was time the Council did something about it.

He got out of his car slowly and, as he did so, the bravado the three pints had given him began to ebb away. But he was here now. He wanted to see her so much, he just didn't care anymore. So what if she sent him packing? He'd get over it. All he knew right then was he had to see her sweet face again.

Her face was still sweet, but it wasn't a happy face. At the sight of him on her doorstep, she became all frowns and pouts. If she was the kind of woman to stamp her little foot, she would certainly have done so.

"What do you want, Barney? Has Pearl left you at last? Is that why you're here?"

Three questions in a row. Shut up Dilys, he said to himself. Just give me a hug. He didn't say that out loud either.

"No, she hasn't left me. But she will. In the meantime, darling, can I just come in for a few minutes. Just for a chat? Please?"

Dilys was a pretty woman, never more so than when she was cross. Or so Barney thought. Her soft brown curls framed her oval face perfectly. Her large brown eyes (like chocolate drops, he always thought) surrounded by long dark lashes, never looked more appealing to him as they did at that moment. Most people would look at Dilys Amory and see an attractive woman in early middle age; pleasing but nothing special. It was true, she was no Jayne Mansfield. But, to Barney, she exuded an air of mystery and sex that no cinema pinup could ever achieve. Dilys was all he ever wanted in a woman, and all he would ever want.

"I suppose you can come in for a few minutes," he heard her say. A few minutes were better than no minutes at all, he told himself.

"Thank you," he said, almost formally. He could see no way of breaking down her resistance.

"Would you like a cup of tea or something?"

Something, preferably. "Er, yes, that would be nice," he replied, sensing there would be nothing stronger on offer tonight.

When the tea was poured, she sat stiffly in the chair opposite to him, smoothing her dress over her shapely knees. "So, how have you been, Barney?"

"You know how I've been. I've been missing you like hell."

She looked down at her smoothed dress and smoothed it some more. "I – I'm sorry."

"Are you?" He leaned towards her and she jerked back, as if repulsed by the very sight of him.

"You know I care about you, Barney. But you're a married man."

"How many times do you have to remind me? Don't you think I know it? I live every day with the knowledge that I'm a married man."

"Well, then. There's nothing more to be said, is there?"

He sipped the tea he didn't want and crunched on the biscuit he wanted even less. Although he had eaten nothing since a sandwich at lunchtime, he found he wasn't in the least bit hungry.

"Can't we at least see each other occasionally? Go to the pictures, maybe? No funny business. Just as friends?"

Dilys sighed and, for the first time that evening, looked as if she was mellowing slightly. But her back was still rigid.

"I don't think that would be a good idea, Barney."

"No, I suppose it wouldn't."

He stood up and stretched. The clock on the mantelpiece told him he should be home now, talking to his wife and being a good husband. But how could he be a good husband to someone who wasn't a good wife? It was unfair. No matter how often he had tried to get on with Pearl, there was a barrier ten feet high between them. That barrier might as well have been constructed of galvanised steel, the distance between them being too great to even make a dent in it. And besides, he didn't want to make up with Pearl. He just wanted Dilys.

He sat in the car and felt like crying. He switched on the radio in time to hear the news. What he heard made him sit bolt upright.

"An item of late news has just been passed to me. The body of a woman in her early fifties was found by the night porter in a fifth floor office this evening at Maxwell's Secure Finance Corporation in the City of London. The police are treating the death as suspicious. Any link with an earlier death in the same building has not been confirmed by the police at this stage."

11

"I heard it on the news last night."

Barney was always pleased to see his friend, Inspector Tony Halliday, but he wished he looked more cheerful. He was obviously a worried man. The sun still shone persistently outside the office windows of Carmichael Investigation Services, but it was having trouble reaching the eyes of his visitor.

"I don't mind telling you we're rattled," said Halliday. He opened a packet of Players and offered one to Barney.

"No, thanks," smiled Barney, a rueful expression on his face. The smell of the smoke as it wafted towards his nostrils was hard to resist. "I'm trying to give them up."

"Sorry, old boy," said Halliday, brushing the smoke away from his friend. "Must be difficult watching me puff away. But I need the nicotine this morning."

"So, another murdered charwoman, then?" Barney leaned forward as if to get the scent of the smoke that Halliday had so thoughtfully flicked away. "Have you any clues?"

"No, not a thing."

"Was it – was it by the same person, do you suppose?"

"What d'you think?" Halliday gave a hollow laugh, followed by a nicotine-laden cough. "Same modus operandi – head in bucket after bashing the poor woman's head in."

"Someone seems to have got it in for cleaning ladies," observed Barney wryly. He stood up and went over to the kettle. It was still only eight-thirty, and neither Muriel nor Jim was there to make a brew. "Coffee?"

"Thanks."

While he waited for the kettle to boil, Barney opened the windows wider. It was already well over eighty degrees in the office. "Aren't there any fingerprints or anything?"

"No – well, not any strange ones. The fingerprints in the offices where the murders occurred have been thoroughly tested. They only belong to the staff."

"What about any new staff? Have they taken on any new people recently?"

Halliday fished out a battered-looking notebook from his pocket and flicked the pages until he found what he was looking for.

"Here we are," he said. "There's one new chap, apparently. Started on a temporary contract basis just over two weeks ago."

"So, was that before the murders?"

"Yes."

"Well, there you are then. Case solved."

"I wish it were that simple."

"Well, surely you've questioned him?"

"Of course. And his manager."

"So – he's not your man, then?"

The kettle whistled cheerfully at that moment, and Barney was distracted as he poured the hot water onto the instant coffee. Returning to his desk, he passed one steaming mug to Halliday.

"Sorry, there's no milk. Muriel brings it in with her. Should be here in a minute if you want to wait."

"No, it's fine," said Halliday, blowing on it. "Need the caffeine as well as the nicotine today."

"Anyway, this new man isn't your man, then?" Barney prompted again.

Halliday shrugged. "Could be, but it's hard to see what his motive could be. Seems a nice enough bloke. In his mid-twenties. Recruited from the States by Maxwell's. He has just the right qualifications for the job, you see. They say no one here has the right know-how. All poppycock, if you ask me. I don't hold with foreign workers taking British jobs."

"But if he *is* the only one capable of doing it?"

"Oh, don't give me that. It's only a risk management role. Any fool can stare into a crystal ball and predict. It's predicting the right outcome that's difficult. And you can't tell me that risk management is infallible. No one predicted the Wall Street crash, did they?"

It was Barney's turn to shrug now. "I haven't a clue," he said, stirring sugar into his coffee. He, unlike Halliday, was missing the milk.

"Well, I don't suppose they did, otherwise it wouldn't have happened, would it? And all the recessions we've had. No one predicted those either.

It's like forecasting the weather. No one can really do that properly. You might just as well hang a bit of seaweed out of the window as listen to those cocky bastards at the BBC."

Barney chuckled. Halliday was definitely in a bad mood today. "I see what you mean. Anyway, to get back to the subject. You've ruled out this chap, then?"

"I have. For the time being, at least. His joining the firm is a mere coincidence. Or so it would appear. Anyway, he's hardly likely to come all the way across the pond just to do in a few cleaners, now, is he? Not with his qualifications."

It seemed logical to Barney too. What would be the point? After all, if the man had it in for charwomen, then why not stay in his own country and murder them there?

Muriel Bird opened the door while he was thinking these thoughts, a welcome milk bottle sticking out from her bag.

"Hello," she said, giving both men the benefit of her pretty smile. She was wearing a light summer frock and little else. Halliday stood politely, appreciating the view.

"Muriel, this is Inspector Halliday," said Barney, grinning as he watched the lascivious look in the older man's eyes. He didn't blame him. His secretary certainly looked a picture today. Her yellow dress accentuated the becoming tan on her arms and shapely legs, and her laughing hazel eyes were enough to melt the hardest of hearts. And both Barney's and Tony's hearts weren't hard at all.

"How d'you do?" said Muriel.

"Tony, this is Muriel Bird, my new secretary."

Halliday took her hand and, for one awful moment, Barney thought he was going to kiss it.

"Is that the milk?" said Barney hastily.

Muriel passed him the bottle. "Couldn't get gold top, I'm afraid."

"Silver's fine," murmured Barney, as he poured the white liquid into his mug.

Muriel made herself a coffee and went over to her desk. Soon the sound of typewriter keys hitting their mark, sometimes missing it, and once or twice getting stuck together, filled the room.

The two men continued to discuss the case, more quietly now. There wasn't much more to say, however, and Halliday soon stood up, ready to depart. He seemed somewhat reluctant to go, however. Barney put this down to Muriel's presence, but there was another reason for the delay which Halliday proceeded to impart.

"The real reason I came to see you, Barney," he said, as he made for the door, "was to ask for your help. I wanted to ask you the other day, but you seemed too preoccupied."

"What – with these murders?"

"Yes, you know." Halliday glanced across at Muriel.

"You can talk freely in front of Muriel," Barney assured him. "She's my *confidential* secretary."

"Oh, right. I won't beat about the bush, then. I need a fresh eye. Another viewpoint. This business has me stumped, I don't mind telling you. I mean, why charladies, for God's sake?"

The typing stopped suddenly. "I was reading about the murder in the paper just now," said Muriel. She had obviously been listening intently to their conversation, even though she seemed absorbed in her typing. "Isn't it awful?"

"Now, young lady," said Halliday, a serious expression on his face. "You mustn't breathe a word of what we've been talking about. The newspapers don't know about the details and we need to keep it that way."

"But why?" Muriel's eyes widened in mock innocence.

"Because we get lots of people confessing to crimes and we need to be able to discount the false leads. It's all so time-wasting."

"Why do people want to confess to something they didn't do?" Muriel looked even more innocent.

"It's because they're barmy," said Halliday.

She laughed. "Must be."

Barney accompanied Halliday to the lift. "I'll be glad to help in any way I can, of course," he said. "Did you have anything in mind?"

The Inspector pulled the lift gates open and stepped into its dark and creaky interior. "Well, it's just a thought. You might be able to keep an eye on the Maxwell's building? I mean, after all the staff have left? I could tell the night porter. Clear it with the powers-that-be and all that."

"I see," said Barney thoughtfully. "But don't you have your own men to do that sort of thing?"

Halliday pressed the down button. "I've been told not to waste too many man hours on these murders. Between you and me, the Yard sees charladies as dispensable. Not important enough to bother with. And the press isn't that interested either."

"I'll have to see if I can slot it into my schedule," Barney shouted, as the ancient lift clanked his friend into the bowels of the earth.

Returning to the office and Muriel Bird, Barney turned over in his mind what the Inspector had said. He couldn't see any way he could watch the place for all those hours. What with the Leon Conrad case, he was up to his eyes. But then, he couldn't work the whole time on the one case, could he? And it would give him an excuse not to be home all the evening with Pearl.

The more he thought about that, the more he warmed to the idea.

12

Pearl Carmichael was a lithe, supple and beautiful young woman. There was no denying those three facts. But she was a selfish, manipulative, ungrateful, jealous and unfaithful one too. Therefore, on balance, she wasn't someone to be completely relied upon. Barney had found that out to his cost.

Marrying in haste and repenting at leisure was not a maxim Barney Carmichael would be likely to subscribe to in the future, having learnt the hard way. When he had first met the lovely auburn-haired Pearl, he had been instantly smitten. She had the type of beauty few men could resist, and Barney was no different. He couldn't believe his luck when he discovered she felt the same way about him. But Barney had a wife at the time even though, like Mr Rochester, he was saddled with one who was certified as criminally insane. Unlike Mr Rochester, however, he hadn't kept her locked in his attic but in various institutions for her own safety as well as for others.

Barney had continued to support and care for his demented wife for many years, but after he met Pearl, he finally took the advice of doctors, family and friends, and divorced her. Pearl and Barney were married as soon as he was free but, after a few happy months, it was soon clear the sort of person Pearl really was. Selfish and demanding, and eventually unfaithful.

She had been determined to leave Barney for Dean Bannister, her partner in their acrobatic act, but it had been Dean who had chickened out in the end. He had quickly dumped Pearl in favour of a former girlfriend, not only as a potential lover and wife, but also as a partner in the act. So Barney, who had been prepared to let Pearl go, was now lumbered with her. It was unsatisfactory for both of them, neither one trusting or caring about the other.

How had it got to this point? he now wondered, parked in the driveway, dreading entering his own home. Pearl would be sitting in the front room, primly no doubt, ready to fire questions at him like 'where have you been till this time of night?' or 'do you think I've got nothing better to do than sit here waiting for you to come home?'

He'd heard it all before. It didn't matter to her that she stayed out half the night herself, rehearsing her new acrobat act and coming home when it suited her. Barney suspected she spent half the night in the pub with her new partners in the act, but he didn't complain like she did. In fact, he preferred it if she was out. He got a bit of peace for once.

Sighing, he got out of the car at last and walked slowly up the path to his front door. There was no light in the hall, and it looked as if the place was in darkness. Good, he thought, as he turned the key in the lock. He was puzzled, though. It was unusual for his wife to be out as late as this. As he entered the house, he heard the urgent bell of the telephone on the shelf next to the front door.

He grabbed the phone just as it seemed to him it was about to stop ringing, sensing instinctively that it was an important call. People didn't ring this late at night just for a chat.

"Is that Mr Carmichael?" came a voice, sounding very far away.

"Yes – that's me." Barney's heart seemed to be jumping in his chest.

"This is St George's Hospital here."

"Hospital?" Barney's worst fears were realized within the space of a few seconds. "Wh-what's happened? Has something happened to Mrs Carmichael?" Poor Daisy, he thought. Poor Jim.

"Yes, I'm afraid it has," said the voice. It was a male voice, soothing and quietly spoken. But to Barney it was as harsh as shattering glass.

"Is – is she – " Barney couldn't bring himself to say the word.

"She's quite comfortable, but she's been asking for you for some time."

"Asking for me? Isn't her husband there?" He couldn't quite see why Daisy would be asking for him unless Jim wasn't available. Where could he be? he wondered.

"Her husband? I don't quite understand. Aren't you her husband?"

"Oh, no," said Barney. Some misunderstanding, of course. "You need to call my brother Jim. I'll give you the number. Hang on." Despite phoning his brother frequently, he could never quite remember his number. He knew there was a '2' in it, and possibly a '7'.

"I don't think so. I'm quite clear she is asking for you. Barnaby Carmichael."

It slowly began to dawn on Barney that it was he who had got hold of the wrong end of the stick. Thoughts of poor Daisy and Jim's predicament had leapt to the forefront of his mind on hearing the word 'hospital'. However, it seemed there was no crisis with them. For the moment, at least. Then he realized.

"Pearl? Something's happened to Pearl?"

"Yes, I'm sorry. She's had an accident while rehearsing. I understand she is part of an acrobatic act?"

Barney sighed. That was one thing he hadn't envisaged. Pearl having an accident. "Yes – th-that's right. What's happened? How bad is she?"

"As I said, she is comfortable at the moment, but she has done some damage to her spine. We can't say at this stage how serious it is."

"Is – is she alone?" Where were her partners in the act all this while? Why hadn't they taken more care of her?

"She is now. Her partners stayed for as long as they could, but they had to go home in the end. We have been phoning you all evening."

"I – I'm sorry, I've only just got home. I'm on my way."

Barney stared down at his wife. Her face was as white as the pillow her head was resting on. She seemed to merge into it, to disappear almost. He would almost have thought she wasn't there if it hadn't been for the black rims around her closed eyes. She looked almost ethereal, as if she was already halfway to the angels.

"Pearl?" he whispered. "It's Barney. I'm here."

Her eyelids fluttered open to reveal two bloodshot orbs, their beauty diminished by pain. "Barney?" she croaked.

He sat down beside her and took hold of her hand. It felt cold and floppy inside his. Tiny as a small bird and just as fragile. He remembered once holding a bird his cat had mauled, stroking it, trying to get life back into it. But it had given a small flutter and departed. He had cried for days afterwards. Pearl's little hand was that small bird. A dry sob escaped his throat, then another.

"What happened, love?" he managed to ask, a surge of tenderness for her welling up inside him. Tears were now making their way down his cheeks. He brushed them away with his free hand.

"I – I fell."

"Why didn't they catch you? What went wrong?"

"It was all my fault. Don't blame Johnny. He'd told me not to go up on the trapeze without him."

"What about – Ben is it? Where was he?"

"He'd gone to the toilet. We were taking a break." Her voice began to crack. She took a deep breath.

"Don't – don't try to speak, love," said Barney now. He kept hold of her hand.

A white-coated figure loomed over them at this point. "Good evening," said the man. "I'm Dr Fisher. I'm looking after your wife. You must be Mr Carmichael?"

Barney released Pearl's hand and stood to shake the doctor's instead. "How d'you do?"

"I think you had better let your wife rest now," said Dr Fisher. Barney recognised the soothing tones of the man who had phoned him earlier.

He turned back to his wife. "I'll come again soon," he told her. "Tomorrow. You must rest now."

The doctor took Barney by the arm and led him out of the dimly lit ward into a small side office. A nurse was making tea.

"Would you like a cup?" she asked him.

When the tea was poured, the young nurse left them alone. Dr Fisher was studying a brown folder, one finger pressed against his lips.

"Hmm," he said. "She fell rather clumsily, it seems." He got up and walked over to a white screen on the wall. He slotted an x-ray into it. "Hmm," he said again.

"Is – is that my wife's x-ray?" asked Barney, standing up to join him.

"Yes," replied the doctor. "You see – there's a vertebra out of place there." He pointed at the offending object. It looked like a jagged white blob to Barney, not a piece of his wife's spine. "And here," continued the doctor, pointing to another white blob. "That one isn't so bad. That should mend without much difficulty."

"But – you're worried, doctor? Will – will she be able to walk when she's recovered?"

"Aye, there's the rub," said the doctor. "I can't honestly say at this stage."

Barney knew before he said it, that would be the doctor's reply. Not the Shakespeare quote – the other bit: *he couldn't honestly say at this stage.*

13

The young man stared at the imposing cathedral situated in the heart of the London he had, up until that moment, only read about in books. It had been Sir Christopher Wren's proudest achievement and he could see why. He had seen pictures of the vast, holy building in the heart of the pulsating metropolis, but the reality surpassed all his expectations.

In fact, the whole city was a wonder to him. New York was a dump in comparison with its overflowing garbage cans, towering blocks of festering people, Latino knife gangs and thousands of different jabbering accents. London was a shining sedate monument to big business, culture and history, going back hundreds of years. To Leon Conrad, this was where he really belonged.

The Bronx was a distant memory to him now. It was relegated to a childhood that had never seemed quite real to him and a mother who had never really cared for him. As he continued to stare at St Paul's, Leon Conrad wished he'd never have to go back to there. He was home now. At last.

The woman he'd called mother (never 'mom') had always been aloof, as if she merely tolerated his existence while she got on with more important matters. He thought of her overpowering scent, scraggy furs with the poor foxes' heads on them and the sunglasses she always wore, fair weather or foul. He was glad he was thousands of miles away from her today.

He still retained a distant memory (was it real?) of a young and lovely woman bouncing him on her knee, singing *Bye Baby Bunting*. She lived here in England, where Bill told him she would be.

Jeanne Conrad had shown little emotion when he'd told her he was going to England to find his real mother, but he knew he'd upset her. He hadn't managed to do that too often, and he was glad. But he knew she wasn't upset because he was leaving her, but simply because he'd found out the truth at last. He had been just another possession to her. She'd always had the upper hand, buying his affections with expensive toys and, as he grew into his teens, expensive cars. Even his own apartment. He'd enjoyed that, but she had made sure it was close by so that she could drop in whenever she wanted to. Just to keep tabs on him.

"You'll be back," she'd told him. "There's nothing for you in England. Not anymore. It's too late. This is where you belong."

That had been just over three weeks ago. Now, standing on the steps of St Paul's, a place he had always wanted to visit, he was crying silently. The discovery he'd made since arriving in London had broken his heart. People were walking past him, in and out of the cathedral, but he didn't care if they saw his tears. Some turned and stared at the obviously unhappy young man, but no one spoke to him.

Back in his hotel room, he sat at the table by the window, the tears still unchecked. He didn't know how it had gone this far. He had only meant to talk to them. Hadn't he? But, if that were the case, why had he gone to all this trouble? He had meant to do *something*. Hadn't he? But surely not that?

He tried to remember, but all he could see was a dark street. It had always been cold but he recalled being happy, happier than all his years in New York where the summers were always intensely hot. The sun always affected him badly, bringing out his unsightly freckles. He was always glad when winter came. In New York.

He looked at the name on the last folder. *Mrs Freda Jenkins*. It gave her date of birth as 1910, making her just over fifty now. The other three had been about that age or a bit older. He was glad he didn't have to deal with younger women.

He thought about Lindsey. She had cried when he'd told her he had to come to London. She had kept asking him why he was going and, if he was determined to, then why couldn't she go with him? They had planned to get married next fall, and they still would, he had told her. But there was something he had to do first. And alone.

He hadn't told her the reason for making the trip. Something had stopped him at the last moment. What if he'd decided to stay in England? If things had turned out as he'd hoped, then he might very well have done that. Of course, he'd have asked Lindsey to come and live with him here, but he couldn't see her leaving her family and friends. She was a home bird, was Lindsey.

He wondered, deep down, if coming to London had been the excuse he had been looking for. The excuse to delay or postpone the wedding. Lindsey was already making so many arrangements and it was over a year away yet. This was mainly down to her mother whom he didn't much like.

His thoughts turned to Bill now. If it wasn't for him, he wouldn't be here. He'd been the only real parent he had ever known, even though he was only the chauffeur and no blood relation at all. Jeanne had made it clear that Bill was a servant. He just drove them where they wanted to go. But he knew he shared her bed sometimes when she was in between other men.

In the early years, Bill had tried to explain why she seemed so promiscuous. She was unhappy, he had told him. She had never got over the car crash in which her husband had died. Only part of that had been true, he had found out just recently. At least it hadn't been the whole truth.

He had only found that out when Bill had been sacked by his mother. Old, fat and unattractive, he was no longer welcome in her life, and certainly not in her bed. She could drive herself around, if she so felt like it, or get one of her numerous men to do that for her. He hadn't even been given a pay-off, rolling in money though she was. He had cried when Bill told him.

"But you're my pop. You've always been my 'pop'. You can't go. I won't let you."

"Don't worry, even though I won't be here every day, I'll always be your pop," he had assured him. "But after what I've got to tell you, you probably won't want me to be."

14

The sun, which had shone almost every day for as long as anyone could remember that summer, sat high in the sky over Blackfriars Bridge. The lunchtime crowds milled over its vast expanse, as the buses hoved to and fro and black cabs weaved in and out around them. Tourists with their cameras leant over the bridge rails gazing down at the River Thames. It was as majestic as they had been told in school, perhaps even more so today with the sun's beams sparkling on the top of its slow-moving waters. The seagulls sat with wings outspread on any available jetties and floating bits of wood. One persistent gull stood, wings outspread, like a statue. The people watching him began laughing, he had been in that position so long.

Muriel Bird was among the crowds this lunchtime. She had a cheese sandwich to eat which she had prepared that morning. When she'd worked at the shipping office she had eaten in the subsidized canteen, but now she worked for such a small concern she had to watch the pennies. But that didn't matter to her. She was determined to become a private detective herself one day. And that day, if she had anything to do with it, would be soon.

But at that moment she wasn't thinking about her job prospects. Today would have been her mother's forty-third birthday, if only she had been around to enjoy it. Muriel sauntered up the dark, shadowy side of Great Bridge Street, appreciating the relative coolness the shade had to offer while her thoughts skittered back and forth over the years.

She had only vague memories of her mother, who had died when she was a small child. A freak accident falling downstairs had carried her off. Just like that. She'd often wondered if her mother had been drunk when it happened but her uncle and aunt, who had brought her up, never went into details.

Despite this early tragedy in her life, she had been happy enough with her aunt and uncle, but less so when her uncle, whom she had dearly loved, died of a heart attack. Her Aunt Ida did her best, but Muriel didn't love her in the same way. She'd married Terry partly to get away from home, although not entirely. She smiled now as she remembered his regular proposals, always on one knee. She liked that, more because the other girls in the office were so envious. Terry was so good looking (he still was) and they'd all had their eyes on him.

Finishing her cheese sandwich now and wishing she'd put some pickle in it, she screwed up the empty paper bag and threw it in the waste bin close by. She couldn't abide litter louts. They made her blood boil. There was one in front of her now. A well-dressed woman in heels much too high for her, judging by the way she teetered on them. Her suit looked like it had been tailor-made for her at Savile Row. What wouldn't she give to be able to dress herself so well? But this woman, despite her immaculate appearance, happily threw down a chocolate wrapper as she ignored the bin conveniently placed within her reach. Muriel picked it up and threw it in the bin, tutting loudly. The woman was impervious, even though she had obviously heard her.

Her life could be worse, she supposed. Terry was a good husband, but there was no getting away from it: he was boring. What she needed was a dose of excitement in her life. The sooner she could do some real detective work, the better.

Muriel looked at her watch now. Two minutes to two. Better get back, she thought. Barney would probably still be at the hospital visiting his wife. What a thing to happen. Poor Barney. Still, it gave her the opportunity she was looking for, sooner than she had expected.

Jim was on the phone to an obviously irate client, judging by the words she heard him uttering as she came into the office. She busied herself making coffee and placed a steaming mug in front of him. His eyebrows rose in gratitude.

Finally, he slammed the phone down and took out his hanky, mopping his brow with it as he took a long slurp. "Bit too hot for this," he said vaguely, leaving Muriel unsure if he meant the coffee or the argument he had just had on the phone.

"Shall I go and get some water from the cooler downstairs?" she volunteered.

"Would you? There's a love."

Returning with two paper cups of water, she sat down at her desk and made a pretence of starting a new pile of correspondence. She drank the water and leaned back in her typists' chair, which swivelled dangerously as she did so. There was obviously a bolt missing, she thought, as she straightened up quickly. That would be the next thing on her agenda of requests: a new chair. Apart from the request she was about to make now, of course.

"Er, Jim …." she began quietly.

"That woman irritates the life out of me. Would you believe it? She tells me the cat that Barney found for her wasn't her Tiddles. I mean, one Tiddles is much like another, surely?"

"There speaks a man who's never owned a cat," she laughed.

He joined in the laughter and drank his water gratefully.

"Er, Jim …." she tried again. This time she was interrupted by the shrill bell of the telephone. She snapped it up with irritation.

"Hello, Carmichael Investigation Services," she said. "How can I help you?" Her voice was polite, if somewhat abrupt.

It was a new client. A woman in obvious distress. She passed her quickly to Jim and took up her handbag. Five minutes' titivating in the Ladies was called for.

All was quiet again when she returned. "Were you able to sort her out?" she asked. "She sounded very upset."

"Her budgerigar has gone missing," said Jim flatly.

"Her budgerigar? I thought at least someone had died."

Jim sighed. "Animals – pets of all kinds – can be great comforts to lonely people. So, I suppose when they go missing or die, they cause just as much upset as a human being dying or going missing. We mustn't be too quick to judge the misery or need of others, Muriel."

"Okay, okay. So, are you going to look for it?"

Jim shrugged. "I said I'd try but didn't promise anything. She asked me to go and see her. I think she's lonely. Probably a widow or something. I said I'd go later when Barney gets back."

"Have you heard how Pearl is?"

"It's not looking good. Barney doesn't think she'll be able to walk again. At least, not for some time."

"That'll put a terrific burden on him, won't it? How will he cope with that and the job?"

"Search me." Jim looked very miserable as he finished his coffee which was much cooler now.

"I might be able to help out."

She let the words settle on the fetid air. She picked up her notepad and tried to fan her sweating face with it. "Can't we get a fan for the office, or something?"

"Good idea. If this weather keeps up, we'll need it if we aren't all going to die of the heat. Anyway, Muriel, you *do* help – a lot."

"Oh, I don't mean typing. I can do that with my eyes shut." Which was true as she was a touch-typist.

"What then?"

She cleared her throat. "These char lady murders – couldn't I get a job at this place as a cleaner myself? Then I could watch what goes on – from the inside."

Jim stared at her. He almost dropped his coffee mug. "You? A char lady. You don't look much like a char lady to me." He laughed.

"Oh, I can look the part, don't you worry. I'm a member of an am dram group. I'm one of their star turns."

"But – I mean, it could be dangerous. And, anyway, how do you propose to get a job there? You can't just walk in and say: here I am. Hire me."

"Well, I think I could easily get a job there. My mum used to work there."

"Really? How long ago?"

"Well, quite a while ago, actually. But I'm sure they'll remember her."

"A char lady? Was she a glamorous char lady then?"

"My mum was very pretty, yes. According to the photos I have of her, anyway. I was very small when she died, so I don't remember her all that well."

"That's a shame," he said absent-mindedly, mulling over Muriel's proposition. Then he spoke with finality. "No. It's completely out of the question. Barney won't wear it, for a start."

"I knew you'd say that," she sniffed, seemingly not unduly perturbed. Which she wasn't. She was going to do it anyway, Barney or no Barney. And then, when she unmasked the char lady killer, the Carmichaels would have to make her a partner. And get another typist.

She smiled to herself as she started to rattle the typewriter keys with some force.

15

Cairo Road looked even more depressing to Barney on his second visit. He parked the car outside number 46 but remained in his seat, despite the sweltering heat inside, even with both front windows fully wound down. They were probably letting in more heat than they were letting out, he realized, but whatever you did in this weather, there was no escaping the tropical conditions that continued to dominate that atypical English summer.

He had been to see Pearl again that morning and he'd found her even more downcast than the day before. It seemed that, with every day that passed, she became more despondent about her situation. Dr Fisher had warned him that her depression wasn't going to help her recovery, and it was down to him, as her husband, to help her 'snap out of it', as he put it. Easy for him to say, Barney had thought. How was he supposed to cheer up a woman who faced the prospect of being a lifelong invalid? A woman that, up until then, had been a lithe acrobat with supple limbs and an almost contortionist-like body. What could he say to her to cheer her up? She wasn't a child of five whose tears he could dry with a lollipop and a comic.

He tried to focus on the reason he was parked in Cairo Road again. After what Jim had said about the renumbering of the houses, and the probable reason for that, he knew he needed to get some answers. The house numbered 42 stood neglected beside number 46, the 'For Sale' sign peeling and dilapidated, as if it had been there for years. Which, he supposed, it probably had. Number 42 was actually number 44, the number he had been given by Mrs Conrad. It was clear something awful had happened in that house and he had to find out what.

He got out of the car which had been posing as an oven throughout the journey, peeling his trousers off the driving seat. His legs were sticking together, making him feel like he had wet himself. He walked up the path to the door of number 46. What was needed was a good thunderstorm to clear the air, he thought, staring up into the sky. It remained stubbornly azure.

Mrs Ridley opened the door almost before the bell had stopped ringing. She had obviously been watching from the front window. That was nothing unusual. Lonely women, stuck at home, spent a lot of time watching the world go by. He felt sorry for them, when he thought about them at all.

"Hello?" It was more of a question than a greeting. The old woman looked at him through red-rimmed eyes. Barney wondered if she'd been crying.

"Hello, Mrs Ridley. Do you remember me? I'm Barney Carmichael, a private investigator." He showed her his card. "I came to see you a few days ago about a missing person?"

She peered at the card, obviously not quite prepared to acknowledge she had recognized him. She took it in her scrawny hand and fished in her apron pocket for her spectacles to take a closer look.

"Do you think I could come in for a minute?" he asked, impatience almost getting the better of him. The heat and Pearl's predicament had put him on a very short fuse. He tapped his foot and ran a hand through his already ruffled hair. People who knew Barney well had never seen his hair tidy yet. It just didn't obey any trichology rules.

She handed his card back and stepped aside with a sniff. "I was about to take a cup of tea into the back garden," she said, almost friendly now. "Would you like one?"

"Just a glass of water for me, please."

This produced another sniff, but the water was provided. Barney took the tea tray from her and followed her through the kitchen into a small paved area surrounded by full blown roses giving off an overpowering scent. There were two metal chairs placed in a shady corner, with a matching table, on which Barney placed the tray. The chairs didn't look too comfortable; in fact, they looked more like instruments of torture than seating equipment.

He gingerly sat down, however, and was surprised to find how comfortable it was, after all. He sipped the water, which was lukewarm like the time before, waiting while the old woman made a palaver out of pouring her tea.

"Now, young man, what can I do for you this time?"

"Do you remember telling me about the houses in this street being renumbered?" he asked.

She looked vague for a moment. "Yes, I think so."

"Right, then, I don't suppose you can tell me *why* they were renumbered, can you? I mean, you said you were here at the time?"

She stared at him over her china tea cup. He noticed the wedding ring on her finger. "I – I'd rather not talk about it, if you don't mind."

That seemed to be a dead end. Barney was beginning to think this second visit was a waste of time, but he ploughed on.

"You mentioned that a young man had come to see you recently who was looking for his mother?"

He studied her closely as she seemed to be racking her brains for the memory of it. "Do you remember telling me that?" he prompted.

She nodded slowly. "Yes. I suppose I do."

"What – what did you tell him? I mean, were you able to help him?" Who could this mysterious man be? He had been looking for his mother. Mrs Conrad was looking for her son and, despite Mrs Ridley seeming to think the man she had met was Leon Conrad, he just couldn't have been. The photo was a reasonably good one, but maybe not clear enough for her. Blind as a bat. Probably all young men looked the same to her, he thought, rather unkindly.

"I – I told him she was dead," she said suddenly.

He hadn't expected that. "So, what did he say then?"

"He asked me if I knew what had happened to her."

"And did you tell him?" It was like pulling teeth. Barney was getting very irritated now. The more he delved into this mystery, the more confusing it all became. He paused, giving himself time to get his temper under control. Taking a deep breath, he began again. "Could you tell me anything about this man? His name, for instance?"

"I didn't ask his name."

Of course not, thought Barney. Why would you? Silly cow. He was getting nowhere.

"Oh, one thing though," she then said.

"Yes?" Barney wasn't hoping for much.

"He had an American accent."

That was too much of a coincidence, surely? Leon Conrad was American. But it couldn't be the same man. Mrs Conrad had clearly stated that her son had come to London to get away from her, so why would the self-same son come to the address his mother had given Barney to find his mother? If it was the same man, he would be assuming his mother was still in the States and, even if she wasn't, he was trying to get away from her, not trying to find her. He put this conundrum on one side for the moment.

"Were you able to tell him anything about his mother? Anything at all?"

"I told him he'd find out how she died from the people she'd worked for."

"Could you tell me who *they* are, Mrs Ridley?"

"No, I jolly well couldn't!" she snapped.

16

Murray Sherman yanked at his tie and pushed the window open as wide as it would go. The heat was getting to him today. He wasn't usually bothered by extreme temperatures at either end of the scale, but his nerves were bothering him and this seemed to be affecting his body's tolerance of the heat.

He was beginning to hate his job. He had come all the way from Brooklyn to take up his post with Maxwell's Secure Finance, but he was slowly regretting his move across the Atlantic. Since being given an office all to himself after his formal induction, he was becoming increasingly aware of a building resentment of his presence. He had even overheard two of his colleagues complaining that he had taken the job that had been meant for someone called Simon. Well, it wasn't his fault, was it? He didn't know. He had applied in all good faith. It had always been his ambition to come to London to work, but things were going wrong very quickly.

But it wasn't only the job. There was all the nastiness about those poor charladies. He was getting suspicious glances as well now. Not only did the people he worked with resent him for taking a post they deemed belonged to someone else, it seemed that now they thought him capable of murder. It was just a coincidence that the murders occurred after he joined the firm. Just a very annoying coincidence.

Still, he could sort of understand why the indigenous staff resented him or were suspicious of him. He'd probably feel the same if he were in their shoes. What he couldn't take was the evil eye he kept getting from that night porter with a face like a ferret. Every time he worked late, he was on the desk when he left. Maybe his work mates could accuse him of being a toady or a swat, but what business was it of a mere desk porter to look down his nose at him? He'd tried saying goodnight to him in a friendly manner, but all he'd got for his pains was an unpleasant curl of the lip and a grunt.

Then, of course, there was that fat Scotland Yard inspector who had questioned him at length about the first murder. He had no reason to suspect him, no reason at all. Just because he worked late sometimes and clashed with the cleaners. He supposed one or other of them had complained to the Inspector and put him on the scent. A very false scent, but that didn't seem to deter him.

He stared out of the window at the street below. There were people out there, wilting, but somehow managing to go about their business. It was lunchtime so it was getting very busy. He liked the buzz of the big city at this time of day, although he had no need to venture out himself as he had brought sandwiches. He saved every penny he could, looking forward to the day when he could buy a property in London. It was where the money was and he had a financial brain, so he should know.

As he continued to stare out of the window, he saw the fat Inspector below, making his way up the steps into the building. He hoped he wasn't coming to see him again. He supposed this second murder had prompted the visit, so he could be seeing anybody in the firm. But no. The knock on his office door soon disabused him of the fact as it opened to reveal Inspector Tony Halliday, looking hot, harassed and irritable.

"Hello, Inspector," said Murray as cheerfully as he could. "To what do I owe the pleasure this time? Guess it's not because I parked illegally." He tried a grin, but Halliday obviously wasn't in the mood for pleasantries.

"You've got that right, sir," wheezed Halliday as he sat down in the vacant chair without waiting for an invitation.

"It's about this second murder, right?"

"Right again. Do you know anything about it?"

"You're very blunt, Inspector," said Murray, the smile that had been playing around his lips disappearing now. "I know absolutely nothing about it. Nothing at all. Zilch."

"Of course, you don't. You work late sometimes, don't you?"

"Yes, sometimes. So do a lot of my colleagues. We're a hard working lot, you know."

"I expect you work a lot harder than your *British* colleagues, though, don't you? I mean, you've got more to prove, haven't you?"

Murray picked up the pen from his desk and screwed the cap back on before replying. The noise of Halliday's wheezing was the only sound in the room for a few moments. "I'm well qualified for my job, Inspector, if that's what you're saying."

"I've no doubt you are. Let's leave your qualifications on one side for the moment. We've established you like to work late sometimes. You told me last time, you sometimes saw the cleaners and they were annoyed because they couldn't clean your office while you were still at your desk."

"Yeah, well, that's certainly so, Inspector. But I'm always happy to move out of the way for them."

"You don't get so annoyed with them that you resort to murder, then?"

"Gee, listen to yourself, Inspector. You're not serious?"

"No, it was a joke."

Sherman's smile returned. Despite everything, he was beginning to quite like the man. "Okay, yeah. I get it. Well, is there anything else I can help you with? I've got work to do."

"We've all got work to do, sir," said Halliday meaningfully. "So, you can't tell me of anything suspicious that you've seen while working late? Anybody hanging around that shouldn't be?"

Sherman thought for a moment. He remembered thinking he'd heard footsteps pass his door one evening, just as he was leaving, but when he stepped out into the corridor there was no sign of anyone.

"No, Inspector, I can't say that I have. But I'll certainly keep a lookout from now on."

Halliday rose creakily, mopping the sweat from his brow with an enormous, none-too-clean hanky. "Thank you. That would be helpful."

"Would you like a cold drink, Inspector?" Murray Sherman suddenly felt sorry for the big man with the impossible task of finding someone in the vast metropolis with a grudge against charladies.

"Thank you," said Halliday, sitting down again. "That would be most welcome."

17

As she had predicted to Jim, Muriel Bird found it easy to get a night time cleaning job at Maxwell's. There was always a need for good cleaners she was told by the personnel manageress, as there were so many offices in the building. Seven floors of them. That amounted to a lot of cleaning.

"I do have another job," Muriel had told her at the briefest of interviews. Cleaners, it seemed, didn't need much in the way of credentials. In fact, it seemed that, as long as she could hold a mop and bucket and knew what to do with them, the job was hers.

"So, it's just for a bit of pin money, is it?" said Miss Malcolm, clearly not interested in Muriel's reasons for wanting to work as a cleaner at the now notorious Maxwell building. *Two down and how many more to go?* had been that morning's newspaper headline.

"Something like that," said Muriel, who had dressed down as best she could for the interview, her usual glamorous self hidden in a shapeless smock dress, and her shiny light blonde hair tied in an unbecoming bun. She had also withheld the lippy and rouge.

"I assume you know about the ..." Miss Malcolm looked embarrassed, shuffling papers and coughing unnecessarily.

"About the murders? Yes, of course."

"And that doesn't bother you?"

"No. I can look after myself. I mean, I can't think of anyone who'd want to murder me anyway."

"Well, the other two ladies seemed perfectly harmless too. There appears to be no motive for killing them, either."

Muriel shrugged. "Well, as I said, I'd like the job if you've no objection to me. My mum used to work here, too. Years ago."

"Indeed?"

"Maybe she was a bit before your time?"

"I'll look her up. She'll be on our files, I'm sure. Bird, that's not a very usual name. Can't be many of them to sift through." Miss Malcolm seemed about to crack a smile, but it wasn't a success. A poker face matched her stiff, poker-like body. 'Flat as an ironing board' as no doubt Muriel's husband Terry would observe were he ever to meet her, which Muriel doubted. Unless, of course, she was the next murder victim. Then Terry would be down on the old bat like a ton of the proverbial for not looking after her staff properly. She smiled to herself at the thought.

"No, that's my married name. My mum's name was Baker."

"Oh, right. Probably a few more of them, but I'll find her, no doubt. Not that I need to bother, I can see you're a trustworthy person."

"And you need all the cleaners you can get." Muriel said out loud which she had no doubt Miss Malcolm was thinking. "But I'd still rather you looked up my mother's details, anyway."

"Very well." There was an almost, but not quite, inaudible sigh. "What was her first name?"

Muriel told her.

"Fine. When can you start?"

After Muriel had left a few minutes later, Miss Rhonda Malcolm looked at the form that her new charlady had completed. Something wasn't quite right, she was beginning to think, although she couldn't put her finger on exactly what it was. Why was that young woman so keen to work here? she wondered. Especially in the circumstances. And why did she make a point of asking her to look up her mother's details? She had only been a cleaner, after all. And Muriel Bird was also only a cleaner now. No need to go overboard checking. They came and they went. Although some were going in a rather violent manner these days.

Perhaps they should take that Scotland Yard Inspector's advice and hire more security staff. For the time being, at least. Until the fiend was caught. Still, she reasoned, the police should be providing protection themselves. They just seemed to mill around for a couple of days with their blue tape, then disappear again. Hardly satisfactory, thought Miss Malcolm.

She slipped the form into a buff folder and wrote Muriel's name on the front. Going to the filing cabinets, she opened the one labelled 'Domestic Staff' and slotted it in place. Oh well, she thought. She was in the 'B's' anyway, so she might as well look up the 'Bakers'. She riffled through the files with expert precision, finding the one she wanted almost immediately.

She stared at the file, and then opened it. It was all too plain to her now why Muriel Bird wanted her to look up her mother's personnel record. All too plain.

18

Barney watched his wife as she slept. Her face against the pillow was still as white as the day before and there was a look of pain in repose which unsettled him. What was to become of her? What was to become of *him*? What was to become of them both?

His future with Dilys was now just a pleasant dream, not a goal he could ever attain. Up until Pearl's accident, he had always hoped she would give him a divorce in the end. But there was no chance of that now. He had been staunchly loyal to his mentally disturbed first wife, even when it was obvious she was psychotic and a danger to herself and everyone else around her. It had been easier, somehow, because he had loved her unconditionally. Pearl, he now realized, had been just a passing fancy. Her beauty had dazzled him for a while, and her seemingly obvious keenness on him had flattered his ego. But they should never have married. Then he wouldn't be in this predicament now, and he'd be free to marry Dilys.

He sat beside Pearl, thinking these thoughts, absent-mindedly eating his way through the grapes in the bowl beside her bed. If only he hadn't been taken in by her. If only he had thought it all through before jumping headlong into a marriage that had turned sour all too soon. It had been Pearl who had first been disloyal, not him. Maybe he would have continued to be loyal to her if she hadn't. The love (or whatever passed for it) would have gone whatever happened, he was sure, but at least he wouldn't be able to blame her for her perfidy. That made standing by her so much harder.

"Penny for them," said a voice above his head.

Barney looked up to see Dr Fisher smiling down at him, complete with white coat and clipboard chart.

"Oh, hello, doctor," said Barney, standing up and shaking his hand. "How – how is she? I didn't want to wake her up, she looks so peaceful." She didn't, actually, but it seemed the right thing to say.

"She's improving very slowly." There was caution in his tone. "But it seems she doesn't have the mental will to get better. Her injuries aren't as serious as we first thought. We have begun some physio already, but she's not responding to treatment."

"It's early days, though, isn't it?" There was a small bird of hope fluttering around inside his chest now. Her injuries were less serious. Maybe that meant she could walk again one day. Right out of his life.

"Yes, it is, but she should be showing some signs of wanting to get better herself. That's what's holding her back. We were hoping to see her walk out of here on crutches, rather than in a wheelchair."

A wheelchair! Barney shuddered. He now had visions of pushing Pearl everywhere, in and out of shops, in and out of the car, in and out of the toilet. No, he couldn't bear it.

"So – when do you think she can come home? I mean, when will she be able to walk about on crutches?" She couldn't come home in a wheelchair, she just couldn't.

"Well, that's just it. There is only so much we can do for her in here. She will attend physio as an outpatient, of course, and hopefully she will get stronger. But I fear she will be discharged in a wheelchair unless she makes a miracle recovery before the end of the week."

"The end of the week? You're discharging her at the end of the week?"

"We must, I'm afraid. The bed is needed for another patient. You'll be looking after her, I take it?" There was a frown on his face as he said this.

Barney held back a long sigh that was threatening to drown out the whole ward. "Yes – yes, of course I will."

"Good man," said the doctor, the frown replaced by a friendly smile. He patted him on the shoulder. "Well, I must get on. I'll leave you to talk to your wife, who I see is just waking up."

Barney turned back to Pearl, attempting a smile as he took her hand. She stirred fitfully, her eyelids opening and closing a few times, before finally focusing on him.

"Hello," she said. "Can – can you help me sit up?"

Barney did so.

"And plump up my pillows."

He did that too, obeying her staccato instructions as if in a dream. This was his life from now on. A nagging invalid for a wife. He would have to do everything for her, day and night. It might have helped if she seemed a little bit grateful to him, although probably not much.

"Comfy now?" he asked, trying to show concern. He had to act the solicitous husband whatever he might feel inside, and what he felt inside at that moment he couldn't even begin to describe.

"No, I'm not. You're very rough."

Rough? He thought. She doesn't know what 'rough' is. 'Rough' is punching her in the face or throwing her around the bed. Or even pushing her out of it. All of which he very badly wanted to do at that moment.

"Sorry," he managed to say. "Are you in a lot of pain?"

"What do you think?"

"Sorry," he said again. "But I'm sure you'll be better soon."

"You think so? You! All you men are the same. You, none of you, know what pain is. You've never had a baby."

Neither have you, he thought. "No, I know. Is there anything I can get you?"

"Oh, get out of my sight. Just leave me alone."

Five minutes later, Barney sat in his car in the hospital car park, tears of frustration edging down his face. 'Leave her alone' she had said. Oh yes, he'd gladly do that. For the rest of her life, if only he could.

19

Barney was in no mood for tantrums. His wife's potential for such outbursts was already preying on his mind, so any tantrums from other quarters weren't welcome, to say the least. The person throwing one this morning in Barney's office, in front of Barney, was Inspector Tony Halliday. He had all the papers under his arm and each one had the same news:

Third Charlady Murdered: Maxwell's in Turmoil
Or very similar. It seemed there was more interest in the murders now that they'd multiplied and looked like increasing. There was a serial killer on the loose. The public, it seemed, liked that idea.

"Do stop pacing up and down, Tony," remonstrated Barney who also had the mother of all headaches to contend with. It was true he had downed the best part of a bottle of whisky the night before, but he refused to acknowledge he was suffering from a hangover. Only alcoholics had those, Barney reasoned. And he wasn't an alcoholic. Although the way the things were going, he might well turn into one if he didn't watch out.

"Sorry – sorry." Halliday slumped into Muriel's swivel typist's chair with all the force of his considerable weight. Barney hoped that when she arrived, she wouldn't complain about the spring having gone. Something had definitely gone, if the sound of 'pinging' and 'squeaking' was anything to go by. His secretary would demand a new chair at once, he felt sure. She was always demanding things, that one. If it wasn't for Jim liking her so much, he'd be inclined to sack her.

"Are you listening to me, though?" demanded Halliday, now thumping Muriel's desk. That too, had seen better days. But at least it was standing up well to the Inspector's hammy fist.

"Yes, yes. You don't have to shout. There's been another charwoman done in. I heard it on the news this morning."

"I don't mind telling you I'm at the end of my tether."

"I bet you are. And this hot weather doesn't help. Apparently, it's set to continue for at least another week according to the weather forecast. There'll be stand pipes in the road soon."

"Look, I don't care about the weather – well, I do. It's too bloody hot. But it's not the point at issue, Barney. What am I going to do? We've got no idea who or what's behind these murders. Not a clue. We don't know where to start and the public want answers."

"Tell me," said Barney, hunting in his drawer for some aspirin, "what are these charladies like? I mean, are they all similar in age, background and so on?" He gulped down the aspirin and glugged water noisily. He poured more into his glass and refilled the Inspector's. He was seriously thinking about getting a small fridge for the office if the heatwave went on much longer. Drinking lukewarm water from the jug wasn't the nicest of experiences. Only necessary.

"Well, yes, they all seem to be similar," said the Inspector, calming down now, and more thoughtful. "They were all in their fifties or thereabouts. This latest one was nearly sixty-two, so she shouldn't even have been working."

"What else can you tell me about them?"

"Nothing much. You know what charladies look like. Crossover overalls, turbans and fags sticking out of the corner of their mouths."

"I thought that was seaside landladies," smiled Barney, his headache easing slightly.

"It goes for charladies too, except they carry mops and buckets to distinguish them."

"I've got a clear mental picture," said Barney, still smiling. "So, in your opinion, they have all been straightforward, ordinary middle-aged women?"

"Yep." Halliday shrugged, pulling his tie loose at the same time. The ring of sweat around his neck was making his shirt collar uncomfortable. He edged a stubby finger in between it and his neck in an attempt to ease the pressure. "Just ordinary women going about their daily – or, in this case, nightly chores."

"And they all work – worked – for Maxwell's?"

"Yep."

"It's very puzzling. I wonder what on earth the motive can be?"

"You've not got any ideas, then?"

"No, I haven't. I – I'm sorry, Tony, I know asked me to do some digging for you, but I've got a lot on my mind at the moment."

"Oh, yes, I heard about your wife. I'm sorry, Barney. I shouldn't be bothering you with this. It's just that I'm at my wit's end. I'm going round the twist. And you can imagine how much pressure we're under from the press. Saying the police are incompetent, that sort of thing. They're having a field day."

"Look, I'll put Jim onto it. We're not far from Maxwell's, and he can easily spend a few hours outside the building keeping watch. I'd do it myself only – well – there's Pearl to look after."

"I know, Barney. I appreciate it. We've detailed men to keep an eye on the place, too, but they can only do so much. So, any help in that direction that you can give would be really useful. As soon as Jim sees anyone going into the building who's not a charlady, let him give me a ring. On my home number if I'm not at the Yard. The way things are going I'll probably still be there at midnight. I think my wife's forgotten what I look like."

Barney smiled to himself. At least he wasn't in danger of forgetting what Halliday looked like himself. He was seeing too much of his friend lately as it was. He hoped the balance would be restored soon. His wife was much more entitled to see the Inspector than he was.

Barney's thoughts turned to other matters as soon as the Inspector had left. He, like Scotland Yard apparently, wasn't really that interested in the fate of a few office cleaners. He had more pressing problems to contend with.

What he was going to do about Pearl was still uppermost in his mind, and the Conrad case wasn't going to solve itself. He looked at the photo of Leon Conrad and wondered where on earth he was. He was dreading his mother turning up, asking for a progress report. What could he say to her? A lot of waffle? She'd soon see through that. She'd probably dispense with his services, and he couldn't really blame her.

In his head, he itemised what he'd found out so far. He could tell her he had visited 44 Cairo Road as instructed, but that it had turned into number 42 somewhere down the line, and that he'd interviewed the next-door neighbour twice, although he hadn't learned a lot (if anything) from her.

He put Leon Conrad's photo back in his wallet and drank some more water. The office was stifling and it was still only ten to nine in the morning. Muriel would be here soon with the milk and she'd make him a coffee and chatter happily about nothing as usual. He supposed he liked having her around, but he wished she'd stop trying to change things.

Everything was all right just the way it was. Except, of course, it wasn't.

20

It wasn't often that Jim's and Barney's day coincided so they were both free at the same time. It was even rarer to be able to grab a pint at the pub at lunchtime together. But today was an exception. A third charlady murder and Halliday's urgent request for help meant things needed to be discussed. Added to that, both men had personal problems that tended to take their minds off their work. This needed to be addressed too, Barney had said firmly as they crossed the road to the already crowded pub.

There was nowhere to sit outside, every table had been taken. It meant they had to settle for the dim and close interior, which didn't help their moods in the slightest. Armed with cool pints, the men searched the bar for a window seat. That, too, wasn't an option. It seemed, even at just after midday, most people had decided to drop everything for an early lunch. The summer heat, longed for all winter, was outstaying its welcome. But at least it was an excuse for skiving, seemingly.

Jim spied an empty table in the far corner at last and made for it with his large strides before anyone else saw it. Barney soon followed with his shorter strides, relieved to be sitting down away from the general hubbub.

"Well spotted, Jim," he grinned, raising his pint to him.

"Now we've got a table, we should order some food," said Jim, swallowing half his pint in one go. "I'm not that hungry. Maybe a salad?"

Barney leaned across to the neighbouring table and retrieved a menu. He picked it up gingerly from the pool of foaming beer which the occupiers of that table had managed to spill. "Mind if I take this?" he asked them politely.

When Jim had been to the bar and ordered their modest salads (and two more pints while he was at it), they sat gloomily silent for several minutes, finishing their first pints before they became too warm to enjoy. Barney broke the silence.

"This Conrad business is driving me mad," he said. "I just don't know where to go from here. I'm dreading Mrs Conrad phoning or dropping in. What can I tell her? We've got to show her something for the handsome retainer she gave us."

"She gave *you*, to be precise," said Jim, obviously peeved that he hadn't seen any of the money himself.

"Oh, don't start, Jim. It's for both of us. It all goes in the books. We're partners. Besides, the cheque hasn't even been banked yet."

"Oh, sorry. Just ignore me."

"It's okay."

"It's not okay. It's like I don't trust you, and you know I do. I trust you implicitly. I always have and always will."

"Don't worry about it."

"Barney – are you paying attention?" Jim watched his brother who seemed to be miles away. He was staring at a pretty girl near the window, but he was sure he wasn't *seeing* her.

"You're worried about more than just this Conrad case, aren't you?" he prompted.

Barney returned his gaze to Jim. "I suppose I am. There's poor Halliday with his dead charladies. They're piling up and being dumped at his door." Barney envisioned the women's aproned bodies leaning against his friend's office door. It almost made him smile. Almost.

"Come off it," said Jim, starting on his second pint. "You don't give a monkey's for those poor women."

"What a terrible thing to say!" Barney glared at him.

"Sorry, but it's Pearl, isn't it? You're worried about when Pearl comes home."

Barney sighed. "Yes, I'm worried. Of course, I am. But that doesn't mean I don't care about cleaners getting murdered all over the place."

"No, I know, Barney. But what are you going to do about Pearl? I suppose you've got to forget about Dilys now, haven't you?"

If he were honest, and Barney was nothing if not that, he knew that was the thing that was bothering him the most. A future without Dilys didn't bear thinking about.

"I can't forget her, Jim."

Jim put out a hand to his brother and gripped him on the shoulder. "You've *got* to. What else can you do?"

"Eat that unappetizing salad, for a start," said Barney, sighting the barman approaching with their food.

They began chomping their way through their plates of drooping lettuce (and very little else) with little enthusiasm. They swallowed their second pints, and Barney went to the bar for two more.

"Three pints is the absolute limit," said Barney with determination. "I don't want to be stuck in the toilet all afternoon."

Jim grinned. "You never could take your drink, could you?" He said this with affection in his tone.

"Anyway, what about you and Daisy. How are things? Has – has she said anything?"

"About the baby, you mean?"

Barney nodded.

"She – she's told me she's pregnant, yes."

"So, it's definite, then?"

"Oh yes, it's definite, all right."

"And what does the doctor say? Should she go ahead with having it?"

"She went to the GP yesterday. She didn't see our usual chap, as he's on holiday. The one she did see said she would consult with an obstetrician, but she wasn't hopeful. Well, that's what I reckon, anyway. Daisy's putting a shine on it, but I know what we were told last time. Nothing can have changed. Apart from anything else, she's getting a bit past it. For child-bearing, I mean."

"You mean she'll be risking her life if she has the baby?"

"That's what I reckon, although Daisy will never admit it."

"So, what did you say to her?"

"I didn't know what to say. I know she won't have an abortion, but that's what they'll recommend when we go and see the specialist next week. It'll break her heart."

"Poor you," said Barney. It was inadequate, but he couldn't think of anything else to say. To tell him not to worry would just be an insult.

Jim blinked back the start of a tear and hid his sadness in his beer glass as he drained the last drops from it. Putting it down, he made an effort. "Anyway, back to business. Oh, I forgot to tell you –"

"Forgot to tell me what?

"Muriel wants to disguise herself as a charlady and investigate from the inside." He laughed. "I could just see your face as she was asking me. I said you wouldn't wear it."

Barney didn't reply straightaway. The idea wasn't such a bad one, was it? Jim sitting in a car outside Maxwell's wasn't anywhere near as effective as being on the inside. And Jim could hardly disguise himself as a charwoman. He'd be tumbled in seconds. With his long limbs, big feet and Adam's apple, even a partially sighted person would tell he was a man.

"You wouldn't wear it, would you, Barney?" Jim repeated.

"I don't know. She could be useful."

"But it could be dangerous. She could get herself killed."

"I think she can take care of herself, that one."

It was the first bright idea to come his way for a long time. If Muriel Bird was determined to vacate her typing chair, then maybe she would make a good private detective instead. Jim wasn't exactly Sam Spade, and what with Pearl and Dilys preying on his mind all the time, it would certainly help to get Halliday off his back if he could prove he was doing something to help.

Of course, if Muriel succeeded in unmasking the killer, she might then demand a pay rise or a partnership, probably both. Could they even afford it? Still, he'd cross that particular bridge when he came to it.

Jim stared at Barney in astonishment. "So, you're going along with the idea?"

"As long as she gets her work done in office hours, what she does afterwards isn't our concern. Is it?"

"I suppose not," said Jim. "But I still think it's too dangerous."

"Because she's a woman? Come off it. Pearl's been on trapezes and high wires for ages. That's dangerous. And – and having a baby's dangerous." He paused. He could have picked a better example, a more sensitive one. But it was none the less true. "Women are facing danger all the time."

Was he trying to convince Jim, or himself? That was something Barney wasn't so sure about.

21

Inspector Tony Halliday, like most of his CID colleagues at the Yard, as well as everyone else in the British Isles, was finding the July heat oppressive. It was getting on his nerves and making him irritable. But irritability wasn't going to get him anywhere, he knew, and he made an effort to keep a lid on his rising temper. It was difficult, as most of the men detailed to work with him on the charlady case were slow on the uptake and tended to be argumentative. They were the kind of policemen who lived up (or rather down) to the disrespectful epithet often applied to them of 'plods'. Sophisticated murderers could run rings round most of them, thought Halliday. And back the other way again.

After his visit to Barney, he decided he had to get a grip on the case. His friend was all very well, but he wasn't much interested in helping him, and he supposed he couldn't blame him. It wasn't his case, after all, so why should he be bothered?

Slumping down at his desk, he pressed the buzzer for a subordinate. The sound, like an angry gnat, finally produced Sergeant Peter Armitage, one of the few colleagues he had any time for.

"Okay, what have you got for me?" he said, hardly bothering to hope for anything at all.

"Something that might interest you, sir," said Armitage, smiling.

Halliday doubted that very much, but he was prepared to be convinced. He slumped back in his chair and looked askance at the younger man. He was tall and well-built, and looked every inch a copper. The kind of copper that featured in boys' comics chasing dastardly villains, all steely blue eyes and square chins.

"Really?" he merely said.

"Yes, sir. I've collated all the statements from the charwomen we got this time and one of the statements, especially, will please you."

Halliday began to sit up. Slumping in Scotland Yard was frowned upon if one did it all the time. The hot weather made slumping almost essential, but he knew the Chief Superintendent, buttoned up in his thick, stifling uniform, wouldn't see it that way.

"Do tell," he encouraged.

"See, this one." Armitage passed him a sheet of paper. "This woman told us about ... well you read it, sir."

Halliday adjusted his glasses carefully. They tended to slip off his glowing, sweaty nose in the dripping heat. Once they were perched at the best angle, he began to read. Reaching the end of the page, he turned it over eagerly. There was nothing more, but it was enough. A pleasurable thrill made its way around his large anatomy.

"So, this woman – what's her name – oh, yes, Freda Jenkins, says she spoke to a young man last night before the murder was discovered? And he had an American accent? I want to speak to this woman. Get her in – now!"

"She's already here. I took the liberty of fetching her. She's in interview room B."

Halliday almost felt like kissing him, but refrained. The heat made people do strange things, but kissing a bloke was just a bit too strange. Instead, he shook him by the hand and clapped him on the back.

"Well done," he said. And, because he could think of nothing else to say, said it again. "Well done."

Mrs Freda Jenkins was sitting in interview room B with a cup of tea, intimidated by her surroundings. Halliday smiled at her. No wonder she looked scared, he thought. The cold, unwelcoming walls of the room seemed to be closing in on them. It may have been tropical outside, but in this infamous little room, which had probably had the likes of Crippen and other evil-doers in it, it could have been the middle of winter.

"Don't get up, Mrs – er, Jenkins," said Halliday kindly, as the old woman scrabbled to her feet. The teacup rattled as she sat down again.

"I – I ain't used to being summonsed," she said, none too politely. Her demeanour seemed to change perceptibly under Halliday's gaze. It was as if she was testing his authority and finding it wanting. He supposed he didn't cut an impressive figure at the best of times, but she would soon know all about it. Time to assert himself, he thought.

"I'm sorry if you have been inconvenienced in any way, Mrs Jenkins, but have you thought you might be next?" He hadn't meant to say that, but something about her manner annoyed him. It had the desired effect, and her former intimidated look returned.

"Gawd, I don't want to end up with me 'ead in a bucket. Why pick on me?"

Halliday wasn't sure if she meant why was *he* or the murderer picking on her. Both, probably.

"Because he seems to pick on women like you, Mrs Jenkins, that's why." He decided she had meant the murderer. "So, any help you can give us to catch the blighter, then the better it'll be for you and your colleagues. Don't you think?"

"I only told the copper last night what I saw. Why d'you want to see me?" She seemed to be getting bolshie again.

Halliday was having some sympathy with the killer now. If Freda Jenkins was his next victim, he wouldn't be surprised, and he wouldn't altogether blame him, either.

"To get the facts," said Halliday as patiently as he could. "You told a colleague of mine that you spoke to a young man last night, sometime before the body of your poor, unfortunate workmate was discovered. Now, is that correct?"

"Yeah, I told you. You got cloth ears?"

This was a disrespect too far for Halliday. "My ears are not made of cloth, Mrs Jenkins, and I'd thank you to keep a civil tongue in your head, otherwise I'll have you up for interfering with the police in carrying out their duty."

A cowed look again. It was like riding a seesaw. When she was high up she looked down on him on the seat below, happy to insult him, knowing he couldn't touch her from there. When she was down below, then she had no choice but to look up to him and behave properly. Up and down, up and down. He was getting giddy.

"Okay. I saw this young man. He'd been working late, but he was just leaving when we arrived. I went into 'is office to start cleaning, but 'ad to wait while 'e collected 'is things, like."

"I see, now we're getting somewhere."

"Can't see where as 'e was going. The murder 'adn't 'appened then, so it couldn't 'ave been 'im, could it?"

"Not unless he doubled back when you weren't looking, Mrs Jenkins." He permitted her a smile now. She wasn't so bad when you got through that prickly surface.

"Suppose 'e could 'ave. I ain't got eyes in the back of my 'ead."

"No, I don't imagine for one minute you have. Now, what I was more interested in was your description of him. And you told my colleague you thought he had an American accent?"

"Oh yeah, 'e was definitely foreign. Could 'ave been American – or Canadian. They sound similar, don't they? Then there's the Irish. They sound like Americans too, sometimes."

Halliday wasn't convinced about the Irish, but he let that pass. "Can you describe him to me, please?"

"Describe 'im? Well, 'e was about twenty-five, I think. 'Andsome too. Fair 'air. Tallish. *'E was nice to me.*" She said this last sentence meaningfully, as if somehow implying that Halliday wasn't.

Halliday's smile widened. The description fitted Murray Sherman perfectly. If she picked him out at an identity parade, then he was halfway home. It only remained to pin the bugger down and make him confess.

Halliday continued to smile as he ushered Mrs Jenkins out of the interview room, already fed up with her. "We will be 'summonsing' you again, I'm afraid," he said. "We will need you to attend an identity parade."

"Identity parade?" The look of horror on her face made Halliday smile even more, but inwardly this time. Serve her right, he thought.

"I ain't attending no identity parade," she said with conviction. "A nice man like that. 'E ain't no murderer, I'm telling you. 'E asked me my name and everything. Said 'e 'oped to see me soon. 'E couldn't 'ave been nicer."

I bet he couldn't, thought Halliday. The swine. Probably marking her out as his next victim.

"Nevertheless, I will be asking you to attend as your civic duty," he said out loud as he took her to the imposing front entrance, winking at the front desk at no one in particular. "Whether you like it or not."

Her answer was a sniff. He watched her departing figure with amusement, mixed with irritation. Still, she was useful, there was no doubt about that. He just hoped she 'did her civic duty' and picked out the right man. If she decided she liked him too much to shop him, that would be another problem, which he didn't even want to admit as a possibility.

But even if Mrs Thingy *did* pick him out, what on earth was the man's motive? Again, it came back to the improbability of someone coming all the way across the Atlantic just to murder a few harmless charwomen. There had to be something more in it than that. There just had to be.

22

Ted Randall had been a porter of some description for most of his working life. Night or day, weekends, even. He'd left school at fourteen and knew his limitations, so was grateful he was always in employment. But his working life spent on reception desks was boring most of the time, and he had to fill the long hours somehow. Despite leaving school at such an early age, he wasn't so dim he couldn't read or write and sometimes he found his work intolerable. If it wasn't for his *Racing Post* and his sixty a day, he thought he'd go potty.

His latest employment, with Maxwell's Secure Finance, was a cut above. In fact, it was the most prestigious job he'd ever had. The office building itself was bigger and grander than any he had ever been in before. Usually, he'd been forced to sit in small cubby holes on building sites, either shivering or sweating, depending on the time of year and the state of the weather. But night portering at Maxwell's was in a different league altogether. As he told his wife, he was going up in the world and no mistake.

His wages, however, were hardly comparable with his surroundings. It seemed that even money-making firms like Maxwell's didn't believe in overpaying its staff. It was the one thing that annoyed him about the job. Otherwise, he was quite content, sitting in comfort all night, making endless cups of tea and picking out the 'certs' for the next day's racing. He always stopped off on the way home for a greasy breakfast at the nearby café before going into Ladbroke's on the corner of his street to place his bets. A routine that was like a religion to Ted Randall. He rarely won and hardly ever even got his money back. But that didn't deter him. One day, he kept thinking, one day he'd crack it.

Then a nice little earner had come his way which had made life perfect for him and his family. Five kids to feed took some doing on what Maxwell's paid him, so the 'nice little earner' was very welcome, even though most of it went on feeding his gambling addiction, rather than his kids.

The nice young man with an accent he couldn't quite place had come in one evening and Ted, doing his duty, questioned the reason for his presence.

"Are you a member of staff, sir? Can I 'ave your name?" he had asked, in all innocence.

The young man, for answer, had tapped the side of his nose.

"Er, may I ask, then, what you're doing 'ere? Do you 'ave an appointment? There's no one on the premises now." He had glanced at the clock above his head, noting it was nearly twenty past eight. Most people had homes to go to, in his experience.

"So, it's your job to check everyone who goes in and out, is it?" the young man had asked. "No one else about?"

"That's right. Just me. Now, if you've got no business 'ere, then I must ask you to leave."

"Now, I kinda think you don't wanna do that. I reckon you could do with a bit of extra dough? I see you follow the horses." The man had noticed the paper on the desk.

"Just an 'obby, that's all. No 'arm in a little flutter now and then." Ted had no idea why he felt he had to justify himself to this stranger.

The young man had smiled at that. "No harm at all. But I guess it wouldn't do you any more harm if you had more dough to do it with?"

The upshot of the conversation was the young man, armed with the key to the personnel offices, entered the lift to the appropriate floor, while Ted Randall pocketed the almost unheard of sum of fifty pounds.

After all, Ted had reasoned to himself, what harm could the man do? He'd asked him where the personnel office was and there didn't seem to be any reason not to tell him. Of course, giving him the key to it wasn't exactly kosher, but he still couldn't see much harm in it. In fact, there had been fifty good reasons not to withhold any information at all from that obliging young man.

Since that night a few weeks ago when he had watched the stranger walk out of the building with some buff personnel files under his arm, he had seen him three more times. Ted Randall would have been a total of two hundred pounds better off as a result, if most of it hadn't ended up in Ladbroke's till.

However, Ted couldn't keep on ignoring the facts that were staring him in the face. He stared at the headline in the evening paper laid out on the desk in front of him.

THIRD CHARWOMAN MURDERED
IN VICIOUS ATTACK
What are the police, doing? Public outcry as
police continue to be baffled

At first, he had dismissed the possibility. It was laughable. Just a coincidence, that was all. The first murder, anyway. It was true the young man had been there that night, the night it happened. But he didn't have a weapon concealed about his person, Ted had been able to tell that just by looking at him. The night had been so warm (it still was), he was in his shirt sleeves. No jacket and he couldn't have concealed a knife or a gun in those tight trousers, that was for sure.

Then, he supposed there were other ways of killing people without using weapons: strangulation, for example. But the press reports didn't say the woman had been strangled. They hadn't said how she'd been killed at all.

And he'd been upset by her death. Old Libby had always passed the time of day with him. She'd given him one of her cigarettes that very evening when he'd realized he'd run out. She was a nice little body. Why would anyone, let alone that young man, want to kill her?

When the next murder had happened a week later, the young man had been there again. The coincidence this time was even more stretched, but Ted wanted to believe in it. After all, that's what coincidences were.

Otherwise they wouldn't be coincidences. Besides, he hadn't liked Sophie so much. She didn't talk to him or even smile when she passed his desk. Bit of a snob, he'd thought. Not that she had any reason to be. No, she was no loss, he'd told himself. And fifty pounds was fifty pounds, after all.

But now there had been a third murder and he had to stop kidding himself. That man, that rich young man who gave him fifty pounds every time he came just to turn a blind eye, was the man responsible for the killings. And this time it was his favourite: Dottie Green. She'd often sat with him before she went home, drinking tea, smoking and chatting, and putting the world to rights. Not any more, she wouldn't, of course. Poor Dottie. Dottie was dead and it was all his fault.

But fifty pounds was fifty pounds. Besides, if he went to the police, they'd arrest him for taking bribes. After all, he couldn't prove the young man had done the murders, could he? Best just to take the money and keep schtum.

23

Muriel started her first evening shift at Maxwell's the following Monday. She had often aspired to working in plush offices such as these, but in a much more senior capacity than the one she had chosen for herself now. A charlady was the lowest of the low, even being a tea lady was slightly better than having to clean out offices and, more galling still, lavatories! Ugh! She thought of her poor mother doing exactly that. But it was different for women back then, she reasoned. That's what they did. That was all that was expected of them.

She had removed her makeup and changed her clothes before turning up at Maxwell's. Her cover would have been blown at once if she'd turned up looking her usual glamorous self. Besides, she rather enjoyed being in disguise and, tonight, she looked every inch a charlady. Her own husband wouldn't have recognized her. Her unbecoming regulation crossover overall hid her slim figure and the scarf wrapped intricately into a turban did its job hiding her pretty hair. She was dowdy enough to blend in with her colleagues now who, she assumed, would be older and plainer than herself.

She felt sorry for women who had no choice but to clean up after other people for a living. They were rarely thanked, just doomed to eke out their existence skivvying, not only for companies like Maxwell's, but no doubt for their own husbands and kids as well.

She entered the office building at six o'clock, an hour before she was officially due to start her duties. She had been called that morning by Miss Malcolm, asking her to arrive an hour early as she wanted to 'discuss a few things'. Muriel wondered what they could be, but wasn't bothered. If it was anything to do with her mother, she knew how to get the upper hand on that score. She didn't intend to use emotional blackmail, however. Unless she had to.

Apart from a few stragglers leaving work for the day, the first person she saw as she entered the building was a weasel-faced individual seated behind the vast reception desk.

"Hello?" said Ted Randall as she approached the desk, his beady black eyes narrowing. "Can I 'elp you?"

"Yes, I'm starting work here this evening," she said, giving him a big smile. "I'm the new cleaner. But Miss Malcolm asked me to come a bit earlier as she wanted to see me first."

"Oh, right," said Ted, looking at a list in front of him. "Mrs Bird, is it?"

"Yes, that's right." She tried to modulate her usually correct grammar. "Er, yeah. That's right," she repeated, hoping to sound more authentic.

He was eyeing her up and down. She noticed a lascivious glint in his eyes and smiled to herself. Not in your wildest dreams, mate, she thought.

"You'll know me again, then?" she grinned. There was no point in upsetting him. She might need his help later.

"Oh, sorry. Yes. I need to know who's supposed to be 'ere and who ain't. Particularly in the circumstances."

Oh, she thought. Yes, that was what was worrying him. Did I know about the murders? Well, I'd have to be deaf, dumb and blind and living in a cave not to.

"Yeah, very worrying," she said. "But I haven't – ain't got a lot of choice. I need the money."

He nodded in what she took for empathy. "I'll tell Miss Malcolm you're here," he said.

Miss Malcolm was sitting bolt upright at her desk as Muriel entered.

"Hello," said Muriel, "you wanted to see me? I hope you're not going to say I can't have the job?"

"Do sit down, Mrs Bird," said the ramrod of a personnel manageress, giving nothing away. "I just wanted to clarify a few things with you first."

"I mean you need all the cleaners you can get at the moment, don't you?" said Muriel, beginning to feel slightly uncomfortable.

"Yes, I suppose we do. No, I don't intend turning you away. I'm sure you'll be an asset to the cleaning staff, being a lot younger than most of them. And probably fitter."

"I hope so, Miss Malcolm," she said politely, relieved that the sack wasn't imminent. It would certainly have been some sort of a record to be dismissed before she had even started.

"I just wanted to talk to you about your mother." Miss Malcolm picked up a glass of water and sipped from it. She didn't offer any to Muriel, even though there was a jugful on the table beside her, together with an extra glass.

"My mother?" Muriel's eyebrows rose and her eyes widened in mock innocence.

"Now don't pretend you don't know what I mean, Mrs Bird."

Muriel could see her mother's file under Miss Malcolm's left hand. It was devoid of rings. She wondered if she'd ever been wanted by a man, or ever been in love with one. She certainly didn't look the type. The steely gaze through her horn-rimmed spectacles was enough to fell a man at twenty paces, she reckoned.

"Look, Miss Malcolm, I know you're concerned. But I just wanted a job. An *extra* job. I've got – well, expenses. Expenses that I can't afford with just my current salary." It was more or less true.

"But I suppose your husband is earning good money?"

Was it any of her business? wondered Muriel. She decided not to antagonize her by voicing this out loud. "Yes, but, well, we're saving up to buy a house, you see. And we'd like to start a family soon."

"So, you won't be with us forever, then?"

Muriel realized her mistake at once. "No, not forever. Who is? But when I say, 'start a family *soon*', I just meant in a couple of years or so."

That seemed to satisfy the martinet who gave her the briefest of smiles.

"So, you're not here to make trouble, then?"

"Trouble?" Muriel was puzzled. "Why should I cause any trouble? I just thought that my mother having worked here once, you'd be more inclined to employ me."

"Look, Mrs Bird, we'd employ King Kong if he turned up with a mop and bucket. The fact that you're Mrs Baker's daughter doesn't make any difference at all." She paused. "As long as you just keep your head down and get on with the job."

Muriel continued to be puzzled. Had her mother somehow got on the wrong side of people when she'd worked there? She'd expected only sympathy when Miss Malcolm discovered who her mother had been. But maybe she'd gone off the rails after what happened. Turned up drunk for work. That kind of thing.

"You need have no worries about that, Miss Malcolm," said Muriel. "As I said, I just need the money and I intend to work hard for it. I'm not afraid of hard work."

"Very well. We'll see how you get on, shall we? I'll take you to meet the others. Now, I don't have to tell you to be extra careful. Don't talk to any strange men. If you see someone still in his office, just go to the next empty one. Don't go in and engage in any conversation. All right?"

"All right. Thank you," said Muriel.

24

"You *must* do what the specialist advises, Daisy."

Jim drove through the hospital gates and parked carefully. There were hardly any spaces left, but he managed to expertly manoeuvre his vehicle into a gap that didn't look quite big enough.

Daisy got out of the car without replying and marched determinedly towards the hospital entrance.

Jim, quickly stopping to lock the car door, soon overtook her. "Are you listening to me?" he demanded.

"I'm not going to kill our baby. *My* baby!"

"So, you'd just rather kill yourself?"

She pushed open the heavy glass door and strode up to the reception desk. Jim, beside her, whispered urgently in her ear. "Do you want Michael to grow up without a mother?"

She stopped in her tracks. The look she gave him made his blood run cold.

"How dare you!" she hissed, pushing him to one side, so that the person behind them could get to the reception desk. "How dare you throw that in my face!"

Jim grabbed her by the shoulders, unrepentant. "How dare I? You ask, 'how dare I'? You know full well that if you go through with this pregnancy that will be the outcome."

She wriggled free from his grasp. "I know no such thing. We haven't even seen the consultant yet."

Jim sighed. It was true. Medical science was improving all the time, finding new cures and new ways to provide better care. But he remained pessimistic.

"Have it your own way," he said grudgingly.

Fifteen minutes later they were sitting in front of a middle-aged man who gave off an aura of white-coated calm and sensibility. Jim wondered if it was the white coat itself that had that effect, or if it was the consultant's own persona that was giving that impression. Either way, it seemed to help calm Daisy too. She squeezed her husband's hand as the man began to speak.

"Good morning," said the man. "I'm Mr Peterson, consultant obstetric surgeon at this hospital. I have your notes here, Mrs Carmichael." He looked at her over the top of his rimless glasses, the only thing about him that Jim didn't quite trust. Rimless specs were somehow suspicious, not quite owning up to being glasses, but not quite disowning the possibility either.

"*Mr* Peterson?" questioned Daisy. "Aren't you a proper doctor, then?"

The man smiled, as if used to being asked this question. "Of course, Mrs Carmichael. I'm a surgeon. Surgeons are all 'Mr'."

Daisy looked sideways at Jim. He could see she didn't understand the distinction at all. He gave her an encouraging smile, but said nothing. He wasn't exactly sure, himself, where the distinction lay. A doctor was a doctor, wasn't he? Be they a general practitioner or one who hid behind a mask and wielded a knife.

"Now, as I said, I've assessed your case, Mrs Carmichael, and I'm afraid it's not good news." He looked suitably serious as he said this.

Daisy's hand squeezed Jim's tighter at this. "What do you mean?" she asked.

"I have to tell you in no uncertain terms that if you go ahead with this pregnancy, you will lose the baby, or be stillborn in the unlikely event it goes full term. We will know better, of course, when we see the scans."

"So, you're saying there's no chance for the baby at all?" said Jim, aware that Daisy was weeping quietly beside him.

"None at all." Mr Peterson, looked away from his patient, while at the same time handing her a tissue. It appeared to be something he had honed to a fine art.

"But I want to try," she said, blowing her nose. "I must try. Isn't there something you can do?"

"Nothing, I'm sorry. You must remember that your last pregnancy gave us all a scare. We were relieved, and not a little surprised, that it turned out so well for both you and the baby."

"But you weren't there last time," Daisy pointed out, not unreasonably.

"No, but the notes are quite clear."

"So, what must happen now?" Jim was getting impatient. The sooner Daisy realized there was no hope, the better, and the sooner she – they – could get on with their lives. They had Michael and that was enough. For him, anyway.

Mr Peterson cleared his throat. "I think the best course now would be to whip your wife in for a termination under general anaesthetic. She will be right as rain in no time."

"Hello. I'm here, you know," Daisy asserted herself. "And the baby? What about the baby?" Daisy demanded.

"Foetus, Mrs Carmichael, *foetus*. Let us not get carried away. It is not a fully formed human being at this stage. Which is good news."

"Good news?" she screamed at him. "What do you mean by that?" She rose from her seat, ready to leave.

Mr Peterson remained calm, seemingly quite detached, despite the obvious distress of his patient. "I'm sorry, Mrs Carmichael, but I can only recommend what I see as your best option."

Jim broke in. "My wife is very much against having a termination, Mr Peterson," he said.

"Are you Catholics?" he asked.

"Er, no, we're not. But my wife can't bear the thought of killing her child. It's understandable, surely?"

Mr Peterson merely nodded. "I sympathise, of course." There was no emotion in his voice, however. "But you must equally understand that if your wife doesn't have this termination, she will almost certainly die and so will the baby. I can't put it more plainly than that. I'm sorry."

Daisy was quieter now, but Jim could see the tears standing in her eyes. The floodgates would no doubt open soon. He reached for the box of tissues on the desk and handed a bundle to her.

"But aren't you going to do some tests, first? To make sure? Blood tests? Scans?"

"Of course, we will do all that, but the outcome will still be the same, I can assure you. The best thing is for me to admit your wife today for the tests, and then for her to have the – er – procedure tomorrow. She can then go home at the end of the week."

Daisy blew her nose and stood up. "I'm going home. Are you coming, Jim?"

Jim raised his hands in despair at the doctor. "I'm grateful to you, Mr Peterson, for your time and your advice. We will think about it and let you know."

"Very well. That's your privilege, of course. But don't wait too long. Time is of the essence in these matters."

"Yes, thank you. I understand."

Jim followed his wife out of the consulting room. "Daisy, you know he's right, don't you?"

"Do I?" She stepped into the lift and pressed the button almost before he had time to join her.

"Daisy, please," said Jim as they bumped down to the ground floor. "What choice do we have?"

"To choose life, rather than death," said Daisy, pushing the exit doors with difficulty.

"But," said Jim, when they were in the car. "If you choose life, you will almost certainly be choosing death, too."

"Don't talk in riddles, Jim. Just drive me home."

Sighing, he turned the key in the ignition, and slowly manoeuvred his vehicle out of the space he had managed to get it into an hour earlier.

25

Third murder, third visit. That figures, thought Murray Sherman. A murder wouldn't be the same without a follow-up visit from Inspector Halliday. He almost looked forward to seeing him now. He smiled as he watched from his office window. There he was, that fat, middle-aged man, puffing and panting up the steps of the building, heading, he was sure, straight for his office.

Of course, he understood why. He was the newest member of staff, an unknown quantity. Before he joined the firm, the charwomen had been safe from harm. Not one of them had met an untimely, unnatural end. The murders had only started after he took up his post at Maxwell's. Ergo, he must be the guilty party. Only he wasn't. But to get that fact through to Inspector Tony Halliday was proving impossible.

Sure enough, not many minutes had passed before the expected knock on his door announcing the arrival of the Inspector.

"Come in, Inspector," he called, sitting behind his desk, doing his best to look serious and imposing, and the least like a murderer as possible. But how did you do that? He'd visited Madame Tussaud's only the other day and had walked around the Chamber of Horrors, fascinated by the exhibits on display. They were all famous murderers, but not one of them looked like a monster. They were just ordinary human beings.

Ordinary human beings who'd done extraordinary things, only not in a good way.

"Hot enough for you?" he quipped cheerfully, as Tony Halliday squelched into the available chair, mopping his brow with a large red hanky.

"If this weather doesn't break soon, I think I'll go mad," he grumbled. "It doesn't help the lift's out of order. Why do you have to be on the fifth floor?"

Murray Sherman shrugged airily. "Could be worse. I could have been on the top floor. Two more floors up."

"That doesn't help."

"Let me get you some water," offered Sherman now, taking pity on him. He brought him a paper cup of cold water from the cooler in the corridor. Halliday gulped it down with relish.

"Thanks," he said. "Now, Mr Sherman, no doubt you know why I'm here yet again?"

"Guess I don't need a crystal ball, Inspector."

"You seem to be treating this business as a joke. I suppose the fate of a few old cleaning ladies isn't of any real significance to a young high flyer like yourself."

Murray Sherman had to admit, to himself at least, that he wasn't much concerned about the fate of the three murdered women. But he stopped short of doing them in himself. It was a complication in his life he didn't need. If only the Inspector could understand that, they'd get on famously.

"I don't have any reason for wanting to kill those poor women," he said, as patiently as he could. He had already told the Inspector that several times. "Please don't think I don't enjoy your visits, Inspector, because I do. But I'm not your man."

"Well, we'll see, shall we?"

"I guess. How can I help you this time?"

"I understand you were working late last night?"

"Er, last night?" Murray paused. His memory wasn't that bad that he'd forget if he had worked late the night before, but the question took him by surprise. Was somebody telling lies about him? He wasn't the most popular person at Maxwell's, but he couldn't think anyone would actually try and frame him for these murders. Unless, of course, the murderer himself was doing so.

"Last night. Less than twenty-four hours ago. It's a simple enough question."

"The answer's simple too, Inspector. I wasn't working late last night."

"I have reason to believe that you aren't telling the truth, Mr Sherman."

Just who was landing him in it? Murray Sherman had always been a team player back in the States. One of the most popular boys at High School and an all-round sportsman too. He had distinguished himself on the baseball field at Yale, as well as academically, and through it all he'd remained a popular guy, a guy most other guys liked being around. Since coming to London, however, all that had apparently changed. Being good at baseball didn't guarantee him a place in the affections of the English, he reckoned, but then it wasn't their national sport. If he'd been a Nobby Stiles or a Bobby Charlton, names he'd heard bandied about since coming to London, things might have been different.

"Okay, Inspector. If you say so. I don't know what I can say to convince you I'm not a liar."

The Inspector sniffed. "I wish I could believe you, Mr Sherman, but my experience in the force has taught me never to take anyone's word for anything."

"Then can I ask who's been telling you I was working late last night? I think I have the right to know."

"I'm afraid you don't," said the Inspector, obviously still uncomfortably hot and bothered.

"Let me get you some more water," offered Murray Sherman.

Halliday stood up, and looked officious. "Thank you, but I'm fine. I need to ask you to attend an identity parade shortly. I trust you will have no objection?"

"Gee, things are getting serious." Sherman thought quickly. Then thought more slowly. Of course. If the person who said he was working late got the wrong man, then the ID parade would only serve to acquit him. On the other hand, if that said person was lying through his or her teeth, the ID parade could be his worst nightmare.

"You will be asked to come along within the next day or so. We'll call you."

"You've got my card?"

"Yes. I've got it."

"Okay, Inspector. I'll look forward to it."

"Will you?"

"Yes, Inspector. I will. I've nothing to fear."

Inspector Halliday returned to the Yard a worried man. To all intents and purposes, Murray Sherman was his man, but he found himself hoping he wasn't. The fact was, he liked the man, and couldn't see him as a killer of innocent women.

"How's the arrangements for the ID parade going, Armitage?" Sergeant Armitage was standing before him later that afternoon with a mug of tea.

"Should have it organized for tomorrow morning, sir," said Peter Armitage, handing over the large mug. "We just need to make sure Mrs Jenkins can attend."

"She'd better. I want this sorted soon as." Halliday took a slurp of the hot liquid. It wasn't much like the tea his wife made. Although he rated his sergeant highly, in the tea making stakes he was precisely nowhere.

"Yes, sir. Do you really think this man Sherman is the killer?"

"It's not my job to *think* a man's guilty. It's my job to *know* he's guilty."

"You don't think he is, though, do you?" repeated Armitage.

"We shall see, we shall see."

"I mean, he doesn't seem to have any motive."

"No. And I can't imagine anyone having a motive to kill innocent cleaners. Mind you, I've been tempted to kill the cleaner who does my office many a time, but then she's a terrible cleaner. Just look at the dust on this." He ran his finger across his desk.

Armitage grinned. "But you wouldn't really kill her, would you?"

"It's come pretty close."

Both men laughed.

26

Muriel Bird glowed with not only the heat, but excitement, the morning after her first stint as a charlady at Maxwell's. Both Barney and Jim tried to show interest in what she was telling them, but their attention wasn't entirely on what she was saying. Barney was more interested in what was going to happen at the end of the week when he brought Pearl home in a wheelchair, while Jim, with Daisy's fate on his mind, was trying hard to concentrate on Muriel's chatter, but not succeeding very well.

"I managed to convince the old bat of a personnel woman that I just needed extra money for a mortgage and so on. I nearly blew it though when I said about starting a family. But I smoothed that over. Besides, they're pretty desperate at the moment. Not many applicants for cleaners at that place!"

Barney laughed politely, nudging Jim who raised enough enthusiasm for a mild titter.

"Anyway, I got on with the other women. They're a gossipy lot, I can tell you. They were a bit cagey with me at first, but I soon won them over." She looked smugly pleased.

"And did you learn anything useful I can tell Inspector Halliday?" asked Barney, consigning his wheelchair-bound wife to the back of his mind for the moment. Muriel was a game girl, he gave her that.

"Er, well, not exactly. The women who were murdered were all quite old, though."

"That's in the papers. Middle-aged and even older," Barney pointed out.

"Yeah, I suppose."

"Did any of the charwomen say they'd met anyone suspicious? Sometimes they don't confide in the police. God knows why, but the lower classes often tend to be suspicious of authority. Even when their own lives could be at risk."

Jim perked up at this. "Lower classes?" he said, his eyebrows raised at his brother. "You're such a snob, Barney."

Muriel interrupted before Barney could think of a suitable retort. "Come on, now. Don't start a row. I know I've not got much to tell you yet, but maybe I'll have more news after tonight."

"Okay, dear," said Jim sweetly. "I'm sure you're doing a grand job. You might even meet the killer. Oh, what am I saying?"

"But I *want* to meet him. That's the whole point of my being there." She grinned at both men, as she busied herself making the morning coffee. "I bought Maxwell House today. In honour of my new job." She laughed. "Not sure it's the same Maxwell's, of course."

"Could be," said Barney. "I understand Maxwell's is an American company, and I know Maxwell *House* definitely is."

"'America's favourite coffee'," quoted Muriel as she spooned it into the mugs. "I've put the receipt on your desk, Mr Carmichael."

Barney picked it up. "Blimey!" he said, before he could check himself. "It's twice as expensive as the other stuff."

"You don't mind, do you?" Muriel seemed deflated. "I thought you'd enjoy the joke."

Barney didn't think it was much of a joke, spending twice as much as necessary. Jim, not in the mood for jokes, didn't find it funny either.

When they all had their expensive coffees in front of them, Muriel brought out her ace. "Oh, by the way, you might be interested to know I'm keeping an eye on the doorman."

Barney looked puzzled. Jim didn't react. "Doorman?"

"Night porter, I think they call him. He was there when I arrived and still there when I left. I didn't like the look of him at all. Face like a ferret. And his eyes are too close together."

"So, do you suspect him of being the murderer?" Barney was almost as enthusiastic as Muriel now. But surely the police would have him on their radar? They must have interviewed him and supposedly ruled him out? Mind you, Tony Halliday hadn't mentioned any night porter to him.

"Ted Randall's his name. Spends all his time drinking coffee and smoking. Oh, and picking out horses in the *Racing Gazette*. Or greyhounds. Not sure which."

"Seems harmless to me," observed Barney. "I mean, you can't accuse someone of murder just because their eyes are too close together."

Muriel stirred more sugar into her coffee. "No, I know that. But there's definitely something fishy about him. I'm sure he knows something, even if he isn't guilty of murder. I'm going to make a special friend of Ted Randall. I think he fancies me, anyway, so it should be easy."

Both men, looking at their secretary now, thought it probably would. She was looking especially attractive that morning, with an almost, but not quite, glimpse of cleavage in the skimpiest of skimpy dresses. At least, that was one thing they could thank the summer heat for.

"Now, just you be careful, my girl," said Jim suddenly. Women all seemed to be on suicide missions these days. "Don't get yourself in too deep. If he *is* by any chance mixed up in this business, and he suspects you suspect him, then you could be in very real danger."

"Oh, I know how to handle myself. Don't worry."

"What does your husband think about all this, by the way?" Barney took a mouthful of his coffee and found it bitter. Had he paid well over the odds for a brand that he didn't even like?

"Oh, Terry's okay. I just told him I'm charring for some extra spending money. And it's true, we *are* saving to buy our own place, so I told him some of my wages can go towards our savings as well."

"So, you haven't told him the real reason you've taken the job, then?"

"Of course, I haven't. He'd hit the roof."

"But he knows the company you're working for, so he must know the danger you could be putting yourself in?" Jim said.

"Oh, I didn't tell him I'm working for Maxwell's. I'm not that daft."

"What if he comes to meet you after you finish? Hasn't he offered to fetch you home? After all, it must be quite late when you leave?"

"Oh, only nine. It's still light then. Besides, we don't have a car, so what would be the point? I'm perfectly okay getting the tube home."

"Oh no, that's not on," said Barney with determination. "Jim or I will meet you at nine o'clock tonight and drive you home."

Muriel giggled. "That's nice of you. So, who's going to be the lucky one tonight, then?"

27

Inspector Tony Halliday had finally abandoned his tie. His shirt was sticking to his back as he entered the lift up to Barney's office. His temper, like the heat, was almost unrestrained. His head was throbbing which, far from finding an added problem, he regarded as a sign the weather was about to break and there was going to be the mother-and-father of a thunderstorm. He had learnt that at his mother's knee. However, his headache had been his companion for the best part of twenty-four hours and the sky remained a persistent blue.

Barney was at his desk when he entered his office, and that pretty blonde was typing diligently at hers. His temper improved slightly at the sight, but not by much.

"Do come in," said Barney with a hint of sarcasm. "We don't stand on ceremony here. There is a door, and it's solid enough to knock on, but no matter." Barney, it was obvious, was in as almost a bad temper as the Inspector.

"What's eating you?" Halliday was in no mood for ceremony of any kind.

Muriel piped up at this fractious moment. "Can I get you a cold drink, Inspector?"

A cold drink? Music to his ears. "Yes, please, dear," he said, smiling effusively. "Have you got a fridge, then?"

Barney pointed to a small white shape in the far corner of the office. "Voilà!" he said. "We're so fed up with drinking tepid water and hot coffee." He had finally succumbed to the expense of a fridge when he realized he couldn't drink the coffee Muriel had bought. The weather forecast also had something to do with it. Another four days at least of unremittingly high temperatures wasn't to be contemplated without the prospect of a cold beer.

"What would you like?" asked Muriel, opening the fridge door. "We've got Coca-Cola, lemonade and some lagers – if you're allowed to drink on duty." She smiled happily at him.

What a treat she was, thought Halliday. Barney had no right to be bad-tempered with such a pretty girl to feast his eyes on all day. All he had was a load of plods, most of whom could audition for the part of Frankenstein's monster and get it. Sergeant Armitage was an exception, of course. Mind you, he wasn't a patch on Muriel Bird.

"One lager won't hurt," he said, taking the can gratefully.

"I'll fetch you a glass. They need washing up," said Muriel.

"Don't bother," said Halliday, "just give me a can opener."

That provided, he sat down carefully in the chair opposite Barney's desk. His own bad temper was at bay now, while he gauged his friend's dark mood. He didn't want to antagonize him any more than necessary, especially knowing the news about Pearl. He decided to start with that.

"How's Pearl?" he asked, glugging his lager noisily.

"No better," said Barney gloomily. "Do you have to make such a noise when you drink?"

Halliday began to wish he had never come this morning. Barney was usually such a tonic when he needed help or advice, or just an ear to listen to his troubles. And his troubles had multiplied since the identity parade that morning.

"Sorry. And sorry to hear about Pearl. Is she at home yet?"

"No. I'm collecting her on Friday."

"And she'll still be in a wheelchair?"

Barney sighed. "Yes. There seems little chance of any speedy recovery."

"Poor woman." Halliday tried his best to drink his lager quietly, but a bubble went up his nose and he began to cough. "And poor you, of course," he added wisely, when he had got his breath back.

"It's a facer, I don't mind telling you. Get me a beer, will you, Muriel?"

They waited while Muriel did the honours. "I presume you'll join the Inspector in drinking out of the can?" she winked.

"Yes, okay. But why don't you go and do the washing up while me and the Inspector have a chat?"

It looked as if she was about to object, but the look in her boss's eye seemed to stop her. She made a noise, however, collecting the dirty mugs and glasses,

151

clattering out of the room with the tray on which they danced precariously.

"Oh, dear," grinned Halliday. "She's not best pleased. Doesn't like doing the washing up. Don't blame her."

"Well, who else is supposed to do it?"

"Okay, Barney. You know what I mean. She doesn't look the menial type."

"She's a woman, isn't she?"

Halliday wished more than ever that he wasn't sitting in Barney's office at that moment. The lager had long since found its way down to his alimentary canal, and no more seemed to be forthcoming. It seemed that only Muriel knew how to open the fridge door.

"Besides, she's getting a bit too big for her boots," said Barney. "Now, what do you want, Tony? I'm a busy man."

They were going to fall out before the day was very much older, thought Halliday, but he still managed to keep his temper in check. After all, he had to take into consideration the strain Barney was under. Looking after a wife in a wheelchair was a prospect he wouldn't relish himself, being used to being waited on hand and foot by his own long-suffering wife.

"I only wanted to update you on the case," said Inspector Halliday. "I've just come from an ID parade."

"An ID parade? So, you've got a suspect then? That's good news." Barney was obviously trying hard to be civil. "Isn't it?" he then questioned, seeing Halliday's miserable expression.

"I thought I had, but apparently I haven't."

"Why? What happened?"

Halliday told Barney about Freda Jenkins and her meeting with a young man at the Maxwell's offices on the night of the third murder. "Her description fitted my main – my only – suspect but, it turns out, it wasn't him. Or so she says."

"Do you think she's lying?" Barney was looking quite interested now.

Halliday shrugged. "Not sure. She seemed to take a fancy to the man she met. Said he asked her name and hoped to meet her again."

"Hmm. Bit ominous. Maybe he's planning to 'meet her again' in order to murder her."

"That's what I thought."

"Oh well, there's nothing you can do. You couldn't hold him, could you?"

"No, I couldn't!" Halliday slammed his chubby fist on Barney's desk. A page or two fluttered up and landed in almost the same place. There was no movement of air. "But the ironic thing is, I don't think he's the killer, anyway. Even though he's my only suspect."

"Sorry, old chap. Fancy a drink this evening?"

Barney was truly sorry for his friend, but his mind wasn't able to think about anything beyond Friday and the dreaded return of Pearl. He just didn't know what he was going to do with her. What if he had to take her to the toilet all the time? Cook for her (he couldn't cook), dress and undress her and, most important of all, be kind to her. All these things were racing through his head, even while the Inspector had been telling him about his suspect and the ID parade. It would have been a fascinating topic at any other time.

And shouldn't he have mentioned what his secretary was doing? She had done two shifts at Maxwell's so far, Jim driving her home on the second evening. Then, he reasoned, what would be the point? Even if Halliday approved of letting a young girl like Muriel get herself into danger, which he was sure he wouldn't, there wasn't anything to report yet. Muriel hadn't come across anyone suspicious so far, apart from the night porter. Maybe he should have mentioned that, but it hadn't occurred to him at the time.

All that aside, he still had the Conrad case to solve. He was fast coming to the conclusion he was a lousy private detective as he hadn't got any further with the mystery. He was thinking about handing the whole thing over to Jim, but his poor brother had his own problems at the moment, as well.

Everything might have been bearable if he could have talked to Dilys occasionally, but she had made it clear he wasn't to contact her in any way – no phone calls, no letters and certainly no clandestine meetings. She had found out about Pearl's accident somehow, he wasn't sure how, and she was even more adamant that his place was with his wife and not with her.

Why did she have to be so moral? Didn't she know she was breaking his heart? And, more to the point, didn't she even care?

28

The dreaded day had dawned, and Barney opened his eyes only to shut them again as soon as he remembered what he had to do at eleven o'clock that morning. He was to collect his wife and bring her home. He rolled over to the side of the bed she usually occupied and lay there as if, by doing so, he could ensure there would be no room for her in the future.

He got up slowly and moved like a dead man to the bathroom. He stared at himself in the shaving mirror and didn't like what he saw. It was someone he didn't recognize. How could he wish his wife away? Wish her dead, rather than here in his home in a wheelchair, glaring at him as if her accident were all his fault? It definitely wasn't. It was those two partners of hers, Ben and whats'is name, who hadn't been looking after her properly.

He cut himself with the razor as he thought about them. Now he would have to greet his wife with fag papers stuck all over his face. His hand was shaking so much, he put down the razor and wiped his perspiring forehead. Another hot day to contend with. Blast it.

Jim had offered to come with him to the hospital, but then who would look after the business while they were gone? Jim had ventured to suggest that Muriel was perfectly capable of answering the phone and taking messages. And if anyone called in person, she'd be able to charm them until one or other of them got back. Barney knew he was right, but where did that leave him? It was almost as if that slip of a girl was taking over. He couldn't let that happen. He was the boss; he'd started the agency because he thought he'd be good at private detective work. That was a laugh. No, he couldn't leave Muriel in charge. His brother had to be there.

But he wished Jim was coming with him, all the same. Maybe they could both have taken Pearl to lunch somewhere, where wheelchairs were accepted, of course. There probably wasn't many of those; he'd often watched young mothers struggling with pushchairs through café doors, wishing they wouldn't bother. Kids and cream teas didn't mix, in his opinion.

He remembered the one and only time he and Dilys had taken tea together. That had been in a quiet, secluded little café not far from where she lived in Finchley. Everything had been fine at first. Tea and scones served, waitress hovering politely in case anything else was wanted. And then two mothers with two yelling two-year-olds strapped into pushchairs arrived, and they managed to circumnavigate themselves to a table where they proceeded to shatter the peace for the rest of their visit. Funnily enough, it wasn't himself but Dilys who'd said, 'kids shouldn't be allowed'.

He thought with fondness of that tea, despite the noisy children. He had learnt even more about the woman he already loved wholeheartedly. Her little quirks, as he began to discover them, only added to her charm.

"I'm not a maternal person," she had told him that afternoon. "I never had children, it just didn't happen. Now I'm glad, what with the divorce and everything."

"But wouldn't you like children?" he had asked her. It was an eye-opener to him that any woman, let alone one so obviously feminine as Dilys, didn't want to be a mother. "What about when we get married? Wouldn't you want a child then?"

She had looked at him for a moment with those big brown eyes of hers. "If *you* want a child, Barney, then I'm happy to." It had thrown him.

"But surely it's *you* who would want one?" She had just smiled at him and stroked his cheek.

"I just told you, love. I'm not a maternal person."

He then thought of poor Daisy going through all manner of hell because she had to have an abortion if she was to survive. But how could she bear to kill her own child? He couldn't begin to contemplate how that must be tearing her apart. It would be the worst dilemma for any woman. But maybe not *any* woman, after all, not if there were more like Dilys. It seemed unnatural, almost cruel, for any woman not to want to give birth. But Dilys wasn't cruel. She was the kindest person he knew, although she wasn't being very kind to him right now. How could she refuse to have anything to do with him? She just couldn't love him the same as he loved her. Perhaps she was a little cruel, after all.

He picked up his razor and tried again. His hand was still shaking but he managed to finish shaving before any more damage was done to his face.

"You look a mess," were Pearl's first words to him when he arrived at the hospital.

Barney looked at her sitting in her wheelchair by her bed which was already made up for the next occupant. He felt like slinging back the covers and tipping her back into it.

"What's happened to your face?" she pressed, her expression blank.

"I cut myself shaving," he told her.

"Tie up your tie," she ordered him.

"It's too hot," he protested.

"I'm not going out of here with you looking like that," she insisted.

Oh, what wouldn't he give to turn back the clock? Barney could see in his mind's eye lovely Pearl on her two equally lovely legs standing at the altar, while he, instead of saying 'I will' was saying 'I won't'. If only. Of course, he would never have done that. He hadn't the nerve for such outrageous behaviour. Hindsight was a wonderful thing, of course. On their wedding day, Pearl had been his heart's desire, and he would have no more left her at the altar than danced naked down the high street with only a cabbage to cover his embarrassment.

He pulled his tie straight and had a go at his hair. That was a distinct failure. The hair on his crown always stood up like Dennis the Menace's.

"Do I look all right now?"

She sniffed. "It'll have to do, I suppose."

"Are you ready to go?"

"Yes. I've seen the doctor. He says I can go."

"Have you got your outpatients appointment with the physiotherapist?"

"Yes. Next week. The card's in my bag. You'll have to make sure you're free to take me," she instructed.

"When is it?" he asked, struggling with the brake on the wheelchair.

"I can't remember," she said blandly.

"Never mind," sighed Barney, finally getting her wheelchair moving. "I'll check later. Do you want to go straight home?"

For the first time that morning, he took in her appearance. Her usually luxurious auburn hair was scruffed back in a bun and didn't look as if it had been washed for a fortnight. Her usually sparkling eyes were dulled as if in pain, either physical or mental, probably both. She seemed to have put on weight too, although she had constantly complained to him that the hospital food was inedible. He supposed lying around all day for nearly two weeks would account for the flab. He suddenly felt deeply sorry for her and vowed to himself to make every effort to try and make her as happy or as content as possible, under the circumstances.

"Well, I'm hardly dressed for the Ritz," she said, breaking into his thoughts.

"No, well. You'll soon be back to your lovely self," he said. He was hoping this was a comforting thing to say, but soon realized his mistake.

"What do you mean?" she snapped. They were now by the car. "*Back* to my lovely self?"

"Er, I just meant – well, your hair needs washing." He might as well be hanged for a sheep as a lamb, he reckoned. He was good at digging himself into holes, and then digging himself in deeper. Getting out of them had always been his problem.

She seemed about to burst into tears. He quickly opened the passenger door and lifted her carefully out of the chair and onto the car seat.

"I hope I'm not hurting you," he said.

"Only my pride," she said. Her threatened tears had gone and in place of them was a beatific smile. He was taken by surprise at this sudden change.

"Oh, I'm sorry, Pearl. You still look lovely, but you've been ill. You can't expect to be back to normal all that quickly. Will – will you need help bathing and everything?"

He didn't wait for her reply. Instead, he folded up the wheelchair and put it in the boot. When he got into the driving seat she was fumbling in her handbag.

"The appointment's next Thursday," she told him, passing him a card. "I'm sorry, Barney."

He wasn't sure if she was apologizing for the fact he would have to take time out of his 'busy' day to take her, or whether it was a general apology for her terse behaviour towards him.

He smiled at her. She had gone through a lot and he had been a pig. He reached over and gave her a hug. She clung to him and this time the tears came.

If only, he thought, he could actually feel *something* for her.

29

The moment Barney had been dreading finally arrived on Monday morning. He had spent the weekend accustoming himself to Pearl's wants and needs, and was feeling shattered. He had persuaded Daisy to come and sit with her while he went to work, but she had done it under protest and had made it very clear to both Barney and Jim that she wasn't to be relied on to do this on a regular basis. As it was, she had to bring little Michael with her and he had set up a howling the moment he had entered Barney's home and seen the wheelchair-bound lady. She must have seemed to him like some weird monster with wheels instead of legs.

Pearl had complained, too, that Daisy was all very well and she was very grateful to her and all that, but the noise of Michael's screams was giving her a headache.

The situation was far from ideal, and needed to be sorted as a matter of urgency. Barney's suggestion of hiring a nurse, or even a home help, had met with equal displeasure by Pearl. She told him she'd rather be on her own than have 'some stranger in the house'.

"But how would you manage on your own?" Barney and Daisy had asked her this question in unison.

"I'll manage," she had said. "Just leave me some food. I can wheel myself to the kitchen."

"Er, yes, but what about – calls of nature?" Barney tried to be as delicate as possible in front of Daisy. He had spent the weekend learning how to manoeuvre

Daisy's inert body on and off the toilet, and it hadn't been a pleasant experience. How could she possibly manage it on her own?

"I'll just have to hold it, won't I? Anyway, you can pop home at dinner time, can't you?"

Could he? He supposed he could. He supposed he'd have to.

So now he was at his desk, and it was half-past-nine on Monday morning. The sun was blaring in through the inadequate blinds onto Muriel's head as she typed. Jim had just arrived and was making the coffee.

"No coffee for me, thanks," Barney had said, just before the knock on the door and the moment he had dreaded had become a reality.

Jim was the first to speak as the visitor entered in a cloud of powder and perfume. Her scent was so strong it stung his eyes.

"Hello," he said. "Can we help you?"

"Jim, this is Mrs Conrad," Barney told him, standing up and offering that lady a chair. He coughed as her scent hit the back of his throat. Muriel was already reaching for her hanky to wipe her eyes which had started to stream.

Mrs Jeanne Conrad gave both men a smile, ignoring Muriel. She sat in the chair provided and crossed her legs in what was obviously a deliberately provocative manner. Her eyes were, as on her previous visit, hidden behind dark glasses.

She was a handsome woman and looked considerably younger than someone with a son in his mid-twenties. At least, Barney thought so. Behind the glasses, however, plastic surgery had gone some way to remove the crow's feet, but in their place was a tightening around the jaw and temple which made her look as if she was about to smile.

"Well?" she began, addressing Barney. "As I've heard nothing from you since my first visit, I thought I'd better remind you of my existence."

Jim turned to the wall to hide a smile. He turned back. "Can I get you a coffee, Mrs Conrad?" he asked.

"What kind do you have? I only drink percolated."

"Only instant, I'm afraid," Barney told her apologetically. "And it's not very nice, either."

Muriel, who had only paused momentarily from her typing when Mrs Conrad had entered the office, looked up at this remark. "Actually, it's very nice, Mrs Conrad," she said. "It's 'America's favourite coffee'."

Mrs Conrad continued to ignore Muriel, whether because she was a mere typist or a mere woman, wasn't clear. "I'll pass on the coffee, thanks," she said to Jim. "Can you fix me a drink?"

"Coca-Cola? Lemonade?" said Barney, eager now to please. If he could at least provide her with a cold drink, she might be a little more amenable to his failure to find her son.

"Gin and tonic, if you have it," she said. Her tone was cool and composed. The hot weather didn't seem to be having any visible effect on her. There was no bead of sweat on her forehead or anywhere else, for that matter.

"Er, we only have lager, I'm afraid." Half-past-nine in the morning, for God's sake, he thought. Was his client an alcoholic?

"Never mind," she said, although her tone left him in no doubt that she did mind. Very much.

"Er, I'm sorry."

Jim only laughed, however. "The sun's hardly peeking over the yard arm yet, Mrs Conrad."

Barney quailed inwardly. But he was surprised to see her smile again and actually laugh.

"You're quite right," she said. "I was forgetting. My body clock hasn't quite gotten used to being on the wrong side of the Atlantic."

The *right* side of the Atlantic, thought Barney. The *right* side.

"Anyway, I won't take up too much of your time. I just wanted to find out what progress you've made in finding my son."

Jim came over to her with his mug of coffee, sipping it as he did so. Barney was astonished how his brother seemed to be treating this obviously fearsome woman so casually.

"You must understand, Mrs Conrad, that London is a big place," Jim told her.

A lesson in geography now was it, thought Barney. He shuffled uncomfortably in his chair.

"Let me get this straight," said Mrs Conrad, still cool and composed. "You're trying to tell me that you have come up with precisely zilch?" She didn't sound angry, but there was an underlying something in her tone now that Barney, at least, took as a danger signal.

Jim, oblivious, continued. "No, Mrs Conrad, we are saying our investigations are ongoing and we're following various leads. Rome wasn't built in a day."

Infrastructure now, thought Barney, quietly hysterical.

"Did you go to the address I gave you?" She addressed Barneynow, turning her elegant figure from Jim.

"I did," said Barney. "It was – well, not very enlightening, I'm afraid."

"Can you be more explicit?"

Barney explained about the number 44 being changed to number 42. He waited for that to sink in before he told her that, according to the neighbour at number 46, her son hadn't been seen at what was now number 42. He hadn't, according to that neighbour, called at her door either. He then mentioned that the neighbour had told him that someone else, another young man, had visited her only recently. He, apparently, had been looking for his mother.

"A strange coincidence, don't you think?" Barney concluded.

Mrs Conrad looked strangely disconcerted now. "Er, yes, very strange."

"I mean, I was looking for your son and this other man was looking for his mother. Both at the same address."

"Yes, quite."

"But we are continuing with our investigations, as my – bro – er colleague, here, just told you," said Barney, hoping he sounded more confident than he felt.

Jeanne Conrad stood. "Very well. You have my contact details. You'll still find me at Claridges when you have something to tell me. Which I trust will be soon."

Jim finished his coffee in a couple of gulps and did a kind of whoop. Barney watched in fascination as he jumped in the air and twirled around. Mrs Conrad had, fortunately, left.

"What on earth's the matter with you, Jim?" asked Barney.

Muriel giggled as she pulled the pages from her typewriter and separated the carbons. "You must have been quite a good acrobat," she observed.

"In my time, Muriel, in my time," Jim laughed.

"Come on, Jim, what's up?" Barney's patience was almost at an end. "What's the jig for?"

"But don't you see? It's as plain as the nose on your face."

Barney's hand automatically went to his nose. Muriel was still giggling.

"The man who turned up at number 42 before you did and the man we're trying to find is one and the same. He's Leon Conrad!"

30

"What are you talking about?"

Jim, his normally sensible brother, the one he could always rely on in a crisis, seemed to have gone completely bonkers. Or so it seemed to Barney. Leon Conrad was Jeanne Conrad's son: that was a given. The mysterious man who had turned up at old Mrs Ridley's was looking for his mother. There was no possible way they could be the same person. He told Jim to get a grip.

Muriel, however, looked thoughtful. "It's quite possible, Barney," she said. "Have you thought that this Mrs Conrad person could be an imposter? Or she could be his stepmother? Not his real mother at all. And Leon Conrad has come to London to find his real mother because he's been told somehow that that's where his mother is. Let's face it, if you had a mother like Mrs Conrad, wouldn't you look for another one?"

"Exactly," laughed Jim. "Muriel – smart girl – has taken the words right out of my mouth."

Too clever by half, thought Barney. But he had to admit she could be right. They could both be right. His powers of deduction had been sadly lacking for some time. Sherlock Holmes, he wasn't. Not by a long chalk.

"That old neighbour said the man we know as Leon Conrad was the man who'd come looking for his mother."

"Yes, I know," said Barney. "But she must have been mistaken Her eyesight's not that good." He took out the photo of Leon Conrad from his wallet and placed it on the desk. He could look like any number of young men. To a near-sighted old woman, at any rate.

All three of them studied it.

"Good looking bloke," observed Muriel, picking it up. "I'd be surprised if this old woman made a mistake. He's quite distinctive looking. More like a film star than an ordinary bloke. Would be nice to find him. I'd quite like to find him myself."

Barney, who wasn't sure what Muriel had in mind if she found him, sighed and returned the photo to his wallet. "I still say she must have made a mistake."

"Look," said Jim now. "I'm at a loose end. Why don't I go and see her? Maybe I'll get more out of her. We need to find out for sure if Leon Conrad was her mysterious visitor."

"Okay. I suppose it can do no harm. I think I got on Mrs Ridley's nerves, so you might have better luck." He often envied his older brother's dark good looks. Saturnine almost. They hardly looked like brothers at all, Barney being fair-haired and on the short side and Jim being dark-haired and lanky.

Barney gave him Leon's photo. "You'd better take it, then."

Jim put it in his pocket and prepared to leave.

"So, you're going now, are you?" said Barney, stating the obvious.

"Might as well. Now is as good a time as any."

"Okay."

"Okay."

Jim found Mrs Ridley at home. She opened the door immediately on his ring. He removed his light summer hat and smiled at her. He had his tie on straight, despite the heat, and he looked the picture of respectability.

"Good morning, Mrs Ridley," he said. "It *is* Mrs Ridley, isn't it?"

"'Ow do you know that?"

"Allow me to present my card," said Jim, still smiling, but already beginning to have reservations about her. Barney was right. Her eyesight did look poor, judging by the almost unfocused stare she was giving him.

She studied it for some time. Jim stood patiently by while she screwed up her eyes behind her spectacles in an effort to read the small print. "You from that same agency as that other feller, then?" she asked at last, looking at him.

"Yes, that's right. Barney Carmichael is my brother, and partner in the business. I wonder if I could have a word with you?"

"If it's about that man 'e's trying to find, I already told 'im I ain't seen 'im."

Jim showed her the photograph. "This is the young man we are trying to find, Mrs Ridley. Are you sure he hasn't been here?"

"I already told the other feller," she said, blinking, owl-like behind her glasses. "That's the bloke who came looking for 'is mother. 'E didn't seem to believe me."

"I see. I don't think he didn't believe you, Mrs Ridley. It's just that we've been asked to trace this man by his mother. So, the man you met couldn't have been this one. Do you see?"

"All I know is that's 'im."

"All right. But do you think I might come in for a moment?" Standing on the doorstep, the sun was beating down on his head, and he was feeling decidedly sick. His hat was no protection at all against its violent rays.

"You'd better." Mrs Ridley looked concerned. He must have gone green, thought Jim.

It was no better inside, however. The parlour was hot and stuffy, despite the open window. Jim felt almost claustrophobic as well as sick now.

"Do you think I might have a glass of water?" he asked her.

"You're just like your brother. 'E only wanted water as well. I make lovely tea."

"I'm sure you do, Mrs Ridley. But it's still so hot, isn't it? I don't really fancy tea right now."

While she was fetching the water, Jim looked through the open window at the pleasant back garden. He saw three cats wandering about, looking as if they owned the place. Cats always looked as if they owned places, no matter where they were, he thought with amusement. Even the queen herself would have a battle on her hands if she tried to remove a cat from her throne when it didn't want to be removed. He'd always wanted a cat, but Daisy couldn't stand them.

172

"I think you should forget all about it, young man," said Mrs Ridley as she handed him the water.

"What do you mean?"

"What I say."

"It's my belief, Mrs Ridley, that there's something fishy going on here." Jim was rattled now. "For example, why was number 44 renumbered? That kind of thing only happens if something awful has taken place in there. Something that must have made headlines at the time. How long have you lived here, dear?"

"Look, Mr – whatever-your-name-is," she said, looking distinctly ruffled. "I've already said more than I should."

Jim wasn't having that. "You haven't told me anything, Mrs Ridley."

She glared at him through her unseeing eyes. "I told that young man – the one in your photo – all that I know. He went away satisfied, so why can't you?"

"Why was he satisfied? What did you tell him that you haven't told me?"

"That's for 'im to know and for you to find out. I've lived here long enough to know when to keep my mouth shut. I don't want any repercussions. I think you'd better go."

Jim was about to protest but she already had him by his jacket sleeve and was beginning to pull him up from his chair.

"Now, it's been nice, and if you feel like calling again – "

"Yes?" enquired Jim, as he was propelled to the door.

"Don't."

Jim removed his hat and scratched his head. He stood outside her front door, not quite sure how he had got there so quickly. Something must have seriously rattled the old girl, he thought.

He was just about to get into his car, when he heard a small, frail voice calling him.

"Young man," it said. "Wait a minute, young man."

He looked across the road to see an old man leaning on his front gate.

"Hello?" said Jim. "Are you talking to me?"

"Yes. Come over here. Don't you take no notice of that daft old bat. You after some information about number 44 as was?"

"Well, yes. In a way."

"Come in here, then."

Jim didn't need bidding twice.

31

Barney clutched the bottle of indifferent red wine in his clammy hand as he approached Dilys's front gate. It was a gamble that was unlikely to pay off, but he had to try. His life was descending from miserable to desperate and it hadn't stopped heading downwards yet. He had chosen the wine carefully, knowing that, in the unlikely event Dilys invited him in and shared it with him, she wouldn't appreciate an expensive bottle. Not because he suspected she had poor taste in that department, but he knew she would feel insulted that he felt he had to 'buy her off' with such things. In fact, she was a woman of such high principles, he wondered if he'd ever be able to match her exacting standards. But he had to try.

As he had predicted before she came home from the hospital, Pearl was being as difficult as possible, finding fault with everything he did and everything he said. He didn't blame her for this, well, not too much. He told himself twenty times a day it was far worse for her than for him. But he did sometimes question if it really was. He couldn't have been more depressed if his house had burnt down and he had been diagnosed with a terminal illness.

So, he had made the decision to try Dilys again. At least she would sympathize with his plight, wouldn't she? She wasn't that hard-hearted – was she? He had a sneaking feeling she probably was, as he rang her doorbell. Maybe he was stupid to still go on loving her so much.

And a moment later, there she was. Standing on the threshold looking as clean as paint. There was no hint of any inner turmoil in her eyes or the set of her mouth. In fact, her mouth was breaking into a little smile and his heart gave a leap of pleasure. Could she be relenting a little?

"Er – hello, dear," he said, hiding the wine behind his back. "I – I couldn't keep away. I'm sorry."

"You'd better come in," she said, her tone neutral. If she was pleased to see him, as the little smile had at first indicated, there was no inkling of her feelings now. The smile, such as it was, had been and gone.

"I – I know I shouldn't have come…." He trailed off, as she obviously wasn't going to argue with him.

"Shouldn't you be at home with Pearl at this time in the evening? Getting her a meal?"

"I – I've been home and done that. I cooked her a shepherd's pie. She threw it at me."

"Oh dear, not much of a cook, then?" The smile was back, but this time Barney didn't get too hopeful.

"No, I'm afraid not. I – I thought I'd better pop out for a bit. Leave her to get over her temper."

"But I presume she still hasn't eaten?"

Barney couldn't have cared less if Pearl had eaten or not. He knew that was wrong, but the shepherd's pie had been perfectly edible, and she could eat the rhubarb tart if she wanted. Unless she wanted to throw that at the wall too. Her shepherd's pie was still where he had left it and he had the unenviable task of cleaning it up to look forward to.

"She – she's got a rhubarb tart," he said lamely.

"What's that you've got behind your back?"

"Er – I – I just thought you and I might have a chat over a glass of wine. Please, Dilys, I need to talk to you. You're my lifeline. Don't turn me away."

She took the wine from him and studied the label. "No expense spared, I see," she said. But she was still smiling.

"I would have got a more expensive one – you deserve the best, you know that – "

"I'm only teasing," she laughed. "I would have been very cross with you if you'd spent too much money on it."

"That's what I thought," he grinned, beginning to relax, even though he was still standing with her in the middle of the hall.

"Come through," she now said.

Her parlour was light and airy, despite the heat outside. He wondered how she did it. But, he reasoned, it was nearly eight o'clock now and the best (or worst, these days) of the sun had gone. Evenings were the best time of the day lately, when people could actually sit out in their gardens and enjoy the balmy weather. It was the midday heat that did for him.

She turned on a corner lamp which gave the room a cosy, intimate look. Barney instantly felt at home. He and Dilys belonged together. His life at home might be miserable, and his work not exactly a success lately, but he could forget all that for the next hour or so.

"How *is* Pearl?" she asked him, as he opened the wine.

"Oh, not good, I won't lie to you," he said, as he glugged the wine into the glasses. "Here's to – " He was about to say 'us' but stopped himself just in time. It was inappropriate. He couldn't say that – not yet. Perhaps not ever.

"Here's to – what?" she smiled, holding up her glass. "Us? That's what you were about to say, wasn't it?"

"Er – well, yes, I suppose I was."

"That's honest, anyway. But you know there can't be an 'us', don't you? Not while you have Pearl. And Pearl needs you much more than I do."

"I know that," he said, miserably, leaving his wine untasted. "Don't you think I know that?"

She placed her hand gently on his knee. It was like an electric shock to him. He had to prevent himself from grabbing it and raising it to his lips.

"You must try and be patient, love," she said. The kindness in her voice made him want to cry.

"But you don't know how awful it all is. How she torments me, day and night. I can't sleep and I can't concentrate at work. I've been asked to find this American woman's son and I don't know the first thing how to go about it. Jim's more on the ball than me – and he's got trouble in his life too. Real trouble."

"Jim? What's the matter with him? Is he ill?"

"No. It's his wife – Daisy. She's going to have a baby."

"But that's not trouble. That's great news – " But she saw Barney's look of despair. "Isn't it?"

"No, it's not. The doctors have all told her she'll almost certainly die if she goes full term. And the baby won't survive either. Or so they are all telling her."

"Oh, that's tragic. I'm so sorry for her. Maybe I could go and see her? Talk to her? What does she intend to do? Have an abortion, I suppose."

"They call it a 'termination' at the hospital. As if that makes it easier. It still means aborting the child. Again, to the hospital, it's not a child but a 'foetus'."

"Yes, I suppose to them it's all in a day's work. So, Daisy has to have an abortion. That's awful, but at least they still have their son – Michael, I think you said?"

"Yes, Michael. My lovely nephew. He's a great comfort."

"Yes."

The silence was only broken now by the ticking of the mantel clock and the clink of their wine glasses.

"What is it, Barney?"

"I don't think she wants to go through with it."

"The abortion?"

"Yes."

"But she must! Otherwise, Michael will have no mother and your brother will have no wife. Surely she can see that?"

"She thinks that if there's a slim chance the child will survive, she must make the sacrifice."

"And bring another motherless child into the world? Doesn't she realize how selfish she's being?"

179

"She doesn't see it like that."

"I know. It must be so difficult for her. But, even if the child survives, have the hospital said anything about the condition it will be in?"

"Condition? Well, no, not as far as I know. Although, now you come to mention it, that would be another reason to have the abortion, wouldn't it? I mean, if the child is born damaged in some way. How would Jim cope?"

"Look, Barney, I think both Pearl and Daisy are being very selfish. And you and Jim are saints for putting up with it."

It was music to Barney's ears, especially to hear Dilys describe Pearl as 'selfish', even though she was a cripple in a wheelchair. He had been trying not to think that himself, but now Dilys had put it into words, he felt vindicated. He'd look after Pearl for as long as he had to, but nothing on earth would make him glad to do it.

"But what can we do about it?" he said, finishing his first glass and pouring them both a second. Her glass was still half full, but he managed to pour quite a bit more in before it overflowed the rim. He saw that the wine was making her speak her mind, and he was enjoying it. This was a side to her he hadn't seen before, and he loved her all the more for it.

"Let me have a word with them," she said, taking a long drink from her glass now. "This wine isn't too bad, you know," she said.

"Yes, it's cheap and cheerful," he agreed. "But you've never met either of them. I mean, they'll probably throw you out for interfering in what doesn't concern you."

She shrugged. "Possibly. Probably. But I do care for you, Barney, and what affects you, affects me. You're sad about Pearl and about your brother's predicament. I can't let that pass without trying to do something about it."

Barney was touched, but he knew it was the wine talking. Besides, she'd never met Pearl and, in the sober light of day, he knew she would think better of it. As for talking to Daisy, he could almost hear Daisy saying it now: 'You haven't had a child so how can you know what I'm going through?' And, to be fair, Dilys didn't know.

"You know you can't do anything, really, don't you?" he said, watching her carefully. He was getting worried, she seemed so incensed. "You're not family – not *yet*, anyway."

That remark seemed to hit home at last. "I know, Barney, I know." She sounded deflated now. "But it's so *wrong!* What both these women are doing. I wish I could storm in there and shake them up for you. And Jim."

They finished the wine between them just as the clock chimed a quarter-to-ten. That cheap bottle of wine had been more of a success than he could ever have imagined. And to think he had nearly chickened out of buying it altogether. What would her reaction be? he had asked himself several times that day. In all his wildest dreams he wouldn't have expected the kiss on the mouth she had given him as he left. The feel of her lips would stay with him for many days to come. He could go home to Pearl now and treat her with sympathy and kindness. He could put up with her moans with a cheerful heart.

He remembered just in time to wipe the lipstick from his mouth as he got in the car to drive home.

32

Jim needed to occupy his mind with something other than Daisy. They had rowed almost constantly from the time they left the hospital, the diagnosis sitting between them like a spectre. But it didn't matter how many times he told her that she would leave Michael an orphan and himself a widower, it made no difference. To kill her unborn child was wrong, whatever the reasons for doing so. That's how Daisy saw it. She had accepted her fate. If she died giving birth, at least the child might survive. And that, as far as she was concerned, was all that mattered.

"But what about Michael?" he had screamed at her, knowing there was no point in mentioning his own plight if she died. He wasn't even in the equation. The fact that he would be left behind to bring up Michael on his own, possibly with a baby (maybe even a handicapped one) had no bearing on the situation. Not in Daisy's eyes.

"I know what's right," she had reiterated until he was sick of hearing it.

"*You* know what's right, you say," he had shouted at her. "Don't you think the medical staff might know what's right too? Even me? Don't you think *I* know what's right?"

"You don't seem to," she had said coldly. "Doctors aren't infallible either."

Jim knew in his heart of hearts that Daisy didn't want to die. She didn't want to leave him and her son.

He suspected she didn't really expect to die at all. The baby would be born healthy and she would survive. She had been to church every day for the past week, lighting candles all over the place and genuflecting like the Roman Catholic she decidedly wasn't. Like so many Godless people, she had turned to God in her hour of need, but Jim knew they needed more than a deity neither of them really believed in to help them now.

But there was no getting through to her. He had left her that morning in tears and it was breaking his heart. He had talked till he was hoarse, but he might as well have saved his breath.

He drove to the newspaper archives hardly concentrating on what he was doing. He braked just in time to save a little boy from going under his wheels. The language that issued from his mother's mouth was something terrible to hear, but he couldn't stop to apologize; he had no stomach or heart for it. He felt like he had no insides at all.

He was a funny old boy, that Gordon Partridge. He had seemed tuppence short of a shilling at first, but then Jim had learned more from him in a few minutes than he and Barney had managed since taking on the Conrad case nearly two weeks ago.

Old Mrs Ridley had been useless. She knew a lot more than she had let on. If she had met Leon Conrad which, to Jim, seemed more than likely now, she had intimated she had told him certain facts that she didn't want to tell him or Barney. He couldn't actually blame her, he supposed. He was almost inclined himself to abandon the case. If Conrad had come to London to find his mother, Jeanne Conrad wasn't being straight with them. For all they knew, he could be running away from her, and the last thing he wanted was interfering private eyes finding him.

But Barney had demurred when Jim had suggested they abandon the case. "We've taken it on, Jim," he had said. "She's given us a generous retainer – more than generous – and I'm honour-bound to carry out her wishes. We must try and find her son."

"But he may not *be* her son," Jim had pointed out.

"We have to find him, whoever he is. Whatever relationship he is to her. Then we've done our job. What she does with the information is up to her."

"I don't like it, Barney."

"No more do I. But we're in no position to turn her down. Or at least we're in no position to turn her *money* down."

Of course, that was true. Money was trickling in from divorce work and lost pets, both activities which Barney had stressed he didn't want to do. Especially not divorce work. He hated it, they both did. Trailing erring husbands or wives to seedy hotels had never been either man's ambition. But it was also true that finding the missing Conrad boy was the most interesting and lucrative case they had had for some considerable time. Another plus was the fact that it wasn't dangerous either. At least they didn't think so. But you never knew in this game.

He thought about what old Partridge had told him. He went over the strange meeting in his mind as he drove through the unfamiliar North London streets.

He had gone over to the old man when he had beckoned him that day (was it only two days ago?) and he had invited him into his home. There was an equally old woman inside, smiling. She had reminded him of Margaret Rutherford, only not so formidable. Jim liked them both immediately, and not just because cold lemonade was on offer by the bucket load.

"You're here about what happened, aren't you?" the old man had begun when the refreshments were served. The chocolate biscuits were as welcome as the lemonade, and the front parlour was the epitome of snug respectability. Jim had felt instantly at home, as if the old couple were his own dear, dead parents. They had been trapeze artists so they in no way resembled the Partridges, but somehow Jim could see in them what they would have been like if they had grown old and not died in that avalanche.

"Er – no," Jim had replied. "I don't understand. I'm here to trace a missing person, that's all."

"A missing person, eh?"

"Yes, that's right. Why – do you know all about it? Have you been speaking to Mrs Ridley?"

"Silly old trout," old Partridge had muttered. "I told her a thing or two. She seems to think it's wrong to drag up the past. But there's wrongs still to be righted. You can help, young man."

Jim, getting on for fifty, could hardly have been described as 'young' but he supposed he was to him. "How?"

"Don't you want to know why number 44 was renumbered?"

That was certainly still a mystery, of course. Maybe that was the key to unlocking the puzzle. Although he couldn't see how. Not then.

"Something terrible happened in there," the old man, obviously enjoying himself, had said without any prompting from Jim.

His wife, meanwhile, had sat by her husband's side on the sofa, nodding and smiling. Her rolls of fat had rippled as she reached out for the lemonade jug to refill his glass.

"Something terrible?"

"Yes – a woman hanged herself in there."

Jim had gasped at that. He hadn't expected something quite so dramatic, but he supposed it made sense. Something like that would put a blot on any suburban landscape.

"It shouldn't have happened," Gordon Partridge had continued, ignoring Jim's gasp.

"No, well, no one should feel it necessary to hang themselves," observed Jim. "Do you know why she did it?"

"Because of the taunts from the women she worked with," Partridge had said without hesitation. "As if she didn't have enough to put up with, without them."

"But why were they taunting her? What had she done?"

"Nothing – that's what she'd done. Nothing! She'd been the victim of a terrible crime herself. You go and read up all about it. It was in all the papers at the time."

"Yes, well, I suppose it would have been. How long ago did this happen?"

"It were a couple of months after the war started – the second one."

"As long ago as that?" Jim had made a note of the date in his pocket diary. 1939. He still couldn't see any connection between Leon Conrad's search for his mother at that address or why Mrs Conrad had given that address as the starting point to find her son.

"When the Blitz came, the street next to this one was blown to smithereens," old Partridge had continued. "Here in Cairo Road, we got away Scot-free. I often say to Ruby," he had smiled at the lady beside him, "don't I, dear?"

Jim had watched the old couple with amusement. It was clear they were still very much in love.

"You do, Gordon," she had cackled, giving him a flirtatious nudge.

"Say what?" Jim had prompted eagerly.

"That it should have been *this* street that got bombed. Then number 44 would have been obliterated. That's what should have happened."

"Well, I don't think your neighbours would have agreed with you at the time," Jim had said, smiling. "But tell me, sir, you seem very wise. You probably

know more about this than the papers can tell me – "
Jim had been anxious to get as much information as
possible, and the old man had seemed ready to give it.
But he had been disappointed.

"That's where I want to stop, if you don't mind."
The old man had shut up like a clam at this point.

"Oh, all right. Er, can you tell me one thing,
though?"

"What's that?"

"Why do you think the woman who hanged herself
in number 44 has any bearing on finding the man I'm
looking for? If it does…"

"You'll find the answer in the newspapers," was all
Gordon Partridge had said. The interview, Jim had
realized, was at an end.

Jim found the newspaper library without much
difficulty and parked without difficulty too. He was
soon attended to by a young, bespectacled woman who
helpfully explained how to use the microfiche.

"Are you looking for anything in particular, sir?"
she asked, as she led him to a microfiche viewer in a
long dark room behind the reception area. Jim was
relieved to find the room cooler than he had expected.
He hadn't been relishing sitting for hours in a hot,
stuffy atmosphere in this museum-like place.

"We're lucky here in the mornings," said the young
woman, as if reading his mind. "The sun doesn't find its
way in here until the afternoons."

She left him to his own devices once he had got the hang of the viewer and he proceeded to scroll through pages and pages and pages, starting from the beginning of 1939. He decided to search as local a paper as possible to cut down on the volume, but there was still masses of material to go through. It was going to take him hours.

It was nearly midday before he had a breakthrough. He was now in November 1939, and there it was. A headline-grabbing account of a young woman who had hanged herself in her Stockwell home. That must be it, Jim thought. A 'eureka' moment and about time. He was hot and thirsty now. The sun was threatening to penetrate the high windows and he needed some fresh air.

He read the piece with deepening concern:

The apparent suicide of a mother of two was discovered yesterday at her home in Cairo Road, Stockwell. The lifeless body of Mrs Doreen Baker, 28, was found hanging by her sister, Mrs Ida Clarke, just after five o'clock yesterday afternoon. Her five-year-old daughter had been collected from school by Mrs Clarke at the request of Mrs Baker and had been left at her home in Brixton, also at the request of Mrs Baker.

Mrs Clarke, 30, considerably upset, said she knew something had been wrong when her sister called to see her yesterday morning, asking her to collect her daughter from school that day. She had stressed to her not to bring her home but to take her to her own home and then come and see her afterwards.

Mrs Clarke said that, although she was shocked at her sister's tragic death, it wasn't a complete surprise to her. Ever since the abduction of her four-year-old son a few months earlier, she had been depressed. She had blamed herself for what had happened as she had been distracted for a few minutes during which time he had been taken. Despite concerted police efforts to find her son, his fate is still a mystery.

Mrs Baker also complained of harassment by her work colleagues who blamed her for losing her son. Mrs Clarke suggested that this was the last straw for her sister.

It is understood that her daughter, who is under the care of Mrs Clarke, will be formally adopted by her aunt and uncle in due course, the child's father having predeceased Mrs Baker.

A formal inquest into Mrs Baker's death is due to be held next Wednesday, 14 November at the local coroner's court.

He read the piece several times. Something was nagging at the back of his mind, something he had read recently. Just now, in fact. He scrolled back through the microfiche. Yes, there is was. He had passed over it, but the gist had sunk in. It hadn't jumped out at him because the incident had occurred in Brixton not Stockwell, but now he read it carefully:

FOUR-YEAR-OLD SNATCHED WHILE MOTHER IN SHOP

Police have launched a nationwide search for four-year-old Derek Baker who was snatched while his mother was in a tobacconist's in Brixton High Street yesterday afternoon.

The mother, Mrs Doreen Baker, 28, is said to be distraught. So far there have been no eyewitnesses as to what happened to the child, but it is understood the police are following up several leads.

Jim stared at the report, still trying to access what was nudging at the back of his brain. The mystery of 44 Cairo Road was solved to some extent – no wonder they had to renumber it. But obviously that hadn't helped to sell it afterwards. It had looked so neglected, and now he knew why. But how did this dreadful business tie up with Mrs Conrad's missing son? If it did at all.

But, Jim reasoned, as he stepped out into the hot August street, it *had* to connect up, otherwise how or why did Mrs Conrad have the address in the first place?

That nudging in his brain became more urgent as he got into his car and found it almost impossible to sit on the searingly hot driving seat. He wound down the windows as fast as he could. His brain wasn't working properly, he knew. He put it down to a combination of the unnaturally hot weather, Daisy's predicament, and a general feeling of apathy about the fate of Mrs Conrad's missing son. He hadn't liked the woman, anyway, and he was even more convinced now that her son should be left in peace. He didn't want to be found and Jim, for one, didn't want to find him.

He drove erratically, trying to breathe. Then the pain in his chest started. Then it was suddenly dark.

33

Barney was still buoyed up after seeing Dilys the previous evening. His good mood was out of all proportion to her kiss, but it had been much more than he could have hoped for, and it was making him more cheerful than he had been for weeks. Jim, by comparison, had descended further into the dumps and Barney was relieved he was out of the office.

He had little hope Jim's errand at the newspaper library would shed any light on the Conrad case. A poor woman's suicide wasn't what they were investigating, was it? And wasn't it a waste of time, anyway? After all, it had happened in 1939, twenty-two years ago. But, let's face it, Barney, he had told himself cheerfully, you've been wrong before.

Today he was determined to be more positive about his work now that his private life had taken an upturn. Where was his relationship with Dilys going now? he wondered. Must be going somewhere, he reasoned, else why the kiss? But he couldn't visualize a future with her, not while Pearl hovered over them in her wheelchair. Metaphorically speaking.

The Conrad case had to be attended to and, while Jim was off on his wild goose chase, he had written out a long and detailed report (detailed, insofar as he kept repeating the same things over again in various different ways to make it seem he was giving every attention to the case) and placed it in Muriel's in tray. He had added in the information Jim had found out as an afterthought, just to pad it out. He was certain that a woman hanging herself all those years ago, even if it was at the same address as Mrs Conrad had given him, had no relevance. But at least she wouldn't be able to accuse him of not investigating properly.

"Can you type that out next, please?" he asked her, as soon as she arrived that morning. "After you've finished the one you're doing now, of course." That was about the missing budgie which had been successfully recovered by Jim in their client's next-door neighbour's garden. Not exactly a mindbender for Sherlock Holmes.

"That about the Conrad case?" she asked.

"That's right."

"But it's not finished. I don't usually type reports until they're finished, do I? Is it a new policy?"

Barney was still unsure of Muriel Bird. She was a definite asset in lots of ways, but she was a cheeky little madam, nevertheless.

"No, it's not a new policy," he sighed. "Just do it."

She glanced through the pages. "It's very long," she observed. "You haven't got very far with the case, so why all this guff?"

"Because I need to prove to Mrs Conrad we're doing something," he said as patiently as he could. "Not that that's any concern of yours. Your job is to type. Okay?"

"Sure," said Muriel blithely. "Whatever you say. You're the boss." Her fingers began to fly expertly over the typewriter keys.

Barney muttered under his breath *she'd do well to remember that* as he opened the fridge and took out a can of lager. The heat was unbearable as usual.

The long morning wore on, and Barney had downed two more lagers. The phone had remained ominously silent. No new clients were clamouring for his services, and the current ones seemed to have lost interest. Barney put it down to the heat.

He began to wonder where Jim was. He'd been gone a long time. Not that he missed him at the moment. He sympathized with him, of course, but there was no doubt he cast a pall over everything when he was present. How could Daisy be so stupid?

He saw that Muriel, having finished the missing budgie report, was now picking up the interim Conrad report. He watched her as she slid the carbons in between the sheets of paper and wound them into her typewriter. She was obviously an experienced secretary, judging by the way she handled the carbons. Whenever he'd try to type something (with one finger) using carbons, they had slithered out of his hands. She knew her stuff, all right. He found it hard to imagine her cleaning Maxwell's offices, and wondered, not for the first time, whether she should be doing it at all. Just how dangerous was it?

The telephone interrupted his thoughts. At last, he thought, a client. About time. He picked up the receiver.

"Barney? Oh, Barney."

It was Daisy's voice, but it was almost unrecognizable through the sobs which seemed to be choking the words out of her.

"Daisy? What's the matter, dear? Has anything happened? Are you all right? Is the baby …?"

All he could hear now were her sobs. Dry, rattling sobs. A soul in despair. He could hardly bear it. She must have had some sort of accident, he thought, which involved losing the baby. Oh God, where was Jim when he was needed?

"It's – it's Jim," she managed to say finally.

"Jim? What do you mean? What's he done? If he's upset you like this, I'll kill him."

"Oh, Barney, no. You probably won't have any need to kill him."

"No need? Well, that's good, then."

"Listen, I'm at the hospital. Jim's been involved in a car crash."

"What?" he screamed. "How – how is he?"

"He's in intensive care. They think he's had a heart attack. While driving."

"Oh God. Was anyone else involved?"

"No, thank goodness. But the car's a write-off."

"What does the hospital say? Is he going to live?"

"Oh Barney. They don't know. They say the next few hours are critical. I'm staying here till I know. They only let me see him for a minute, but he was unconscious. Please come, Barney. I can't face this alone."

"I'm on my way. Which hospital?"

"The Middlesex. Please Barney – please hurry. I couldn't bear to lose him."

Muriel, having been told to 'hold the fort', was doing just that. Poor Jim, she thought, as she absent-mindedly battered the typewriter keys. She hated typing. It bored her rigid. The sooner she proved herself a good private detective, the better.

Then her eye caught the address. 44 Cairo Road. She typed on. Something had happened there a long time ago, and it had been renumbered 42. Something awful. Her face was as white as the paper she was typing on.

34

After several false starts, Barney managed to find his way along the dark corridors of the hospital, their walls painted a forbidding yet vivid blue (to hide stains?), to a door marked 'Relatives' Waiting Room'. Opening the door, he was relieved to find the walls painted in a more restful, pale green. A colour more conducive to receiving bad news, he supposed.

He didn't see her at first. All the chairs were empty. Then he saw her standing by the window in the corner. Although the sun continued to shine outside, the position of the window in the waiting room managed to avoid the worst of the heat and blaring light. Daisy Carmichael's figure was shrouded in darkness, no doubt matching her mood.

She turned as Barney approached her. "Hello, Barney," she greeted him, her voice flat.

He took her hand and kissed her cheek. "Hello, dear," he said. "I'm so – so sorry. Is there any news?"

"No, not yet. All I get is cups of tea and wary smiles," she said.

He noticed two empty plastic cups on the table where several magazines were arranged. Unopened. How relatives, waiting for news of their loved ones, could read at a time like that, passed Barney's comprehension.

"Is – is he going to be all right?" The thought of life going on without his big brother beside him wasn't to be contemplated.

Daisy shrugged. "They don't know."

"Where is he now? Can I go and see him?"

"He's being wired up to machines. They said I could come and see him when he was settled."

"I don't understand it," said Barney, sitting down. Daisy came and sat beside him, the view out of the window obviously of less interest now. "He had a check-up only last week, didn't he?"

"Yes," she replied.

"And they said he was okay? Fit?"

"Yes."

"Then why?"

"It's my fault. It's all my fault." She suddenly burst into tears. "I've been so stupid! So selfish."

"How – how, Daisy? How can it be your fault?" He patted her hand which felt cold to his touch.

"I should have agreed to the termination straightaway. It was worrying the hell out of him – losing me. I was prepared to die, Barney, can you believe that? I wanted to give birth to a baby I wouldn't be able to bring up. And leave Jim and Michael. How could I have been so stupid?"

Barney handed her his none-too-clean handkerchief. "Come on, Daisy, you needed to be sure. You needed to be sure there was no other way. It's a big thing. Abortion."

"I hate that word," she said, blowing her nose and offering the hanky and its contents back to Barney.

"Do keep it," he said hastily. "Abortion? Yes, it's a dreadful word. Termination – that doesn't sound so drastic, somehow."

"But it amounts to the same thing."

"Yes, but terminating a pregnancy for medical reasons is different from having an abortion because you don't want the baby. All the difference in the world."

"You're right, of course. That's why I've agreed to have the – termination." She looked in danger of crying again. Barney looked down at his shoes which, like his handkerchief, were none-too-clean.

"I'm glad, Daisy. For your sake, as well as Jim's."

"But all that worry has led to his heart attack and now I'm afraid I won't get the chance to tell him what I've decided."

He put his arm around her. "You *will* get the chance," he said with determination. "He *will* recover. My brother is as strong as an ox."

But did he believe it? Did he think Jim would pull through? In his heart of hearts, as he held Daisy now sobbing uncontrollably, he didn't believe he would.

The door opened a few minutes later. They pulled apart to see a nurse standing there. She wasn't smiling.

"You can see your husband now, Mrs Carmichael. But only for a few minutes," she said.

Barney stood up. "Is he – is he conscious?"

"Who are you?" Her tone wasn't particularly friendly. Barney thought nurses were meant to be kind and sympathetic. But apparently not. Not this one, at any rate.

"I'm his brother."

"He is conscious, yes. But he mustn't be excited. So, you can see him after Mrs Carmichael." She permitted herself a little smile now. Barney smiled back. After all, it couldn't be very nice to have to deal with distraught relatives when you had seriously ill patients to deal with too.

When it was Barney's turn to see Jim, he suddenly felt scared. He'd never seen someone who'd suffered a heart attack before. Would he look different? Would his features be distorted? No, he told himself. That was strokes, wasn't it?

And he was relieved to find Jim looking much the same, apart from the wires attached to him and a beeping machine.

"Hello, Jim," he said quietly. "How are you feeling?"

"Rotten," croaked his brother. Barney was overjoyed to see him smiling, however.

"I take it Daisy has told you the good news?"

"Good news?"

"About the termination…"

"Hardly good news. But, yes. She's told me."

"So, she's going to be all right. And so are you."

"I don't know. I don't feel …."

Barney picked up the water glass on the bedside table and put it to Jim's lips.

Jim gulped down the water and gave a little cough. "Thanks. Look, Barney, I found out quite a lot at the newspaper library."

"Don't worry about that now," said Barney quickly. He had strict instructions not to excite the patient, and Jim was getting agitated.

"In my inside pocket. My jacket." Jim's eyes were focused on the bedside cabinet. "In there."

Barney opened the cabinet door and drew out Jim's outdoor clothes. He found the jacket and pulled out the wallet in the inside pocket as instructed.

"Open it," said Jim, looking feverish. "Quick, before the nurse comes back."

Barney opened it. Inside were two photostat copies of newspaper articles.

"When you've read them, you'll know a lot more. I think I can see a connection between them. Something that links our investigation to them."

Barney gave him some more water. "Please, Jim, don't excite yourself. Please. I'll read them. Don't worry."

"Good, good." Jim's raised head fell back on the pillow, exhausted.

"I'd better go now. That nurse is a bit of a tartar, isn't she?"

Jim seemed about to laugh, but coughed instead. "She's efficient, though."

"She'd have to be."

Barney and Daisy left the hospital together, and he gave her a lift home. Instructing her to sit down, he put the kettle on for tea.

"Have you got someone who could come in and be with you for a while?" he asked her when the tea was brewed and poured out. He handed her the sugar bowl. "Good for shock," he advised. He could do with a strong, sweet tea himself.

They sat and drank the tea in silence.

"Have you?" he asked again.

"Have I what?"

"Got someone who can come in? Be with you. So you're not on your own."

"I'll be fine, Barney. Don't fuss."

"All right, then. I'll be back later to take you back to the hospital."

"Thanks, Barney. You're a darling."

"I know." He grinned at her. She grinned back.

Barney studied her pale, drawn features. She was plumper these days, but still pretty. This latest setback hadn't helped, of course.

"He'll be all right, Daisy. You'll see."

"Will he?"

"Yes, I'm sure he will." He said the words, but he wasn't convincing either Daisy or himself.

35

The one thing Leon Conrad had was money. Lots of it. As soon as he had arrived in London, he'd withdrawn nearly a thousand pounds. He hadn't needed so much, but he suspected, rightly as it turned out, that Jeanne Conrad would freeze his account. Once she knew he had gone, he knew she'd be spiteful enough to do it. She would starve him out into the open, if necessary. Like a hunted animal. But he'd beaten her to it and had enough to live on for weeks. As long as necessary, in fact.

He'd had a piece of good luck in finding Ted Randall at the reception desk. He was exactly the type, you only had to look at him. That weaselly face, those tiny black eyes set too far into his head. The eyebrows meeting in the middle of his forehead, giving him a permanent frown. Skin and bone too. Just ripe for bribery, and Leon had plenty of money for that.

It had been easy right from the start. Ted had handed over the key to the personnel office in exchange for the money. There would be a lot more where that came from, Leon had told him. It had taken him only about twenty minutes before he'd found what he was looking for. The filing cabinet marked 'Domestic Staff' had helped enormously, as he'd had visions of wading through hundreds of files in order to find what he was looking for.

That had been the first time. This was to be his fifth and final visit to Maxwell's. He was glad. He was sick of the place. He checked in his wallet now. There was the fifty pounds packaged to give to Ted to join the two hundred he'd already been given. That would be the lot. Once he'd bought Randall's silence for the last time, he would be through. After that, he'd have to go back to the States and to Lindsey, whether he wanted to or not. He couldn't stay now. He couldn't risk getting caught. Marriage to Lindsey wouldn't be so bad. He could live with her. Living with himself was going to be the problem from now on.

Bill had once told him how Jeanne Conrad had gone to pieces after her husband had died. This knowledge had served to make him more patient with her than he otherwise would have been, and he had tried to like her, oh how he had tried. But what he hadn't been told was that her four-year-old son had died in that crash too. Leon had been a substitute, not her real son at all.

It had all come out after Bill had been sacked. A broken man, he had told Leon everything. It seemed that, after the tragic accident, Jeanne had wanted a complete change. So, they had travelled to England, and to London. For a while she forgot her troubles at the night clubs and casinos that were flourishing in Soho at the time. It was only two months or so before Britain was to declare war on Germany, but you would never have known it, Bill had said.

"She seemed to be getting over her loss, but then she saw *you*".

Leon had been a four-year-old English boy, trailing around with his doting mother but, when Jeanne Conrad saw him for the first time, his fate was sealed. Bill had been driving her around South London on that hot July day, and he had had to confess to her that he was lost. They had been making for some museum or other, he couldn't remember which, and somehow they had found themselves in Stockwell. Mrs Conrad had been finding the heat oppressive, and she had kept badgering him from the backseat as they drove up and down the London streets. It was only when she saw the little boy that she stopped complaining.

Bill remembered the name of the road and the house number as if it were yesterday. Jeanne had seen an exact replica of the son she had lost come out of that house.

"Jeanne had insisted I drove at a discreet distance to see where you were going. You clung on to your mother's hand as she went into shop after shop, then the library, then the park."

It had been all too easy, said Bill. "There you were, wandering out of the tobacconists. Alone. Your mom was inside the shop. You had ice cream all down your sailor suit. There was no one else around. I pulled up and Jeanne opened the car door. You were inside in seconds. I drove away to the sound of your screams. It was pitiful to listen to you. I loved you from that moment. I secretly vowed to do everything to make you happy."

"It you had wanted me to be happy," Leon had told him through his tears of disbelief, "you would have returned me to my mother."

"I wanted to. I tried everything to make her bring you back. But I was her employee. I did what she told me."

"Even when you knew what you were doing was wrong?"

"It was difficult for me. I felt sorry for her and – because, I suppose, I wanted to keep you too. But I worked for her and she paid me. Well, I had to make a living."

"So, you brought me back to the States and left my mother to break her heart."

Bill had hung his head at that. "I'm sorry, Leon. I wish I could turn back the clock. I devoted my life to your mother's whims and look how she's repaid me. I only wanted what was best for her – and for you. She never stinted on giving you what you wanted. And you were happy, weren't you? Despite everything?"

And he supposed he had been. At least until he had found out his real mother was on the other side of the Atlantic. All that Bill had told him about his abduction was a complete blank to him. The trauma of that day must have blotted out all memory of it.

And if all that hadn't been enough, Bill had then dropped another bombshell. "You had a sister, too. She was a little older than you."

He hadn't been able to take this in. A sister? Someone he had never known. Someone he would probably now never know. A vague memory had flitted through his mind at her mention, but it had been nothing tangible. Since the moment Bill had told him about her, he had tried to conjure her up, but without success.

"She was a pretty little thing," Bill had recalled. "We saw you and your mom drop her off at the school gates."

"Do you think I'll ever find my mom and sister again?" he had asked him. But Bill hadn't any hope to give him, only a London address. 44 Cairo Road. As he had made his way to the plane, he'd turned and waved at the old man. He looked so frail, standing there. Somehow, he knew he'd never see Bill again. Just one more thing to make him sad.

He'd had such hopes when he'd landed at Heathrow. But, as it turned out, all he'd got for his pains was a dead mother and an end as dead as she was. The old woman who had lived next door to his mother at the time had told him what had happened to her and what had led to her suicide.

It had been a shock, but he was getting used to shocks now and he'd no time to dwell on his own feelings. He'd have to sort them out later. His mom's brutal death had to be avenged and he had a sister to find. The old neighbour was sorry not to be able to help with that, although she remembered there was an aunt. She'd thought that the little girl had gone to live with her, but she'd had no idea where that was. It could have been Timbuktu for all the good it would do him.

However, she was able to tell him, somewhat reluctantly, where next to go. The end hadn't been quite so dead after all.

It was enough. There was some satisfaction to be found in revenge. A dish served so cold, it was almost frozen.

36

"Oh, it's you. To what do I owe the pleasure? You don't often honour me with your presence."

Mrs Ida Clarke stared at the young woman on her doorstep. A pretty sight she was too. Her blonde hair tied back from her neck, giving her an elegant Audrey Hepburn-like appearance, delicate feet in strappy sandals, white linen, figure-hugging slacks, sleeveless top and nails polished to perfection matching her lipstick. Her suntan emphasized the unusual hazel of her eyes. Muriel Bird looked as if she had just come off the catwalk and the admiring glances she'd received on her journey to her aunt's home in Willesden left her in no doubt how attractive she was.

However, Ida Clarke wasn't so impressed. "When did you last deign to visit me?" she asked her, as she stood aside to let her in. "I think the last thing I got from you was a Christmas card."

Muriel didn't rise to the bait. She knew her aunt only too well. She had lived with her from the age of five and, although she was fond of her, she wasn't immune to her faults, which were many. If ever there was a more cantankerous woman than her aunt Ida, she had yet to find her. But she supposed blood was thicker than water.

"Anyway, I repeat. To what do I owe the pleasure? You haven't just dropped in for a chat. I know you."

"How about putting the kettle on?" was all Muriel said to these jibes.

"You and Terry still all right? You haven't had a bust up, have you?"

"No, of course not."

Ida Clarke busied herself with the kettle while her niece sat down at the kitchen table and watched her.

"Hot enough for you?" Ida asked rhetorically, spooning tea into the teapot.

"I manage to keep cool, thanks," said Muriel, answering her anyway. Her aunt had never been much interested in how she was feeling.

"It's too much for me," said Ida, sitting down herself while she waited for the kettle to boil. "Plays havoc with my chilblains, this weather."

"Really? I thought it was the cold weather did that."

"Fat lot you know."

This banter, not entirely friendly, was typical of the kind of relationship they had always had. There was love in there somewhere, even though it was rarely acknowledged by either woman.

When the tea was poured, neither of them really wanting it, Muriel cleared her throat. "What really happened to my mother?" she asked.

Ida Clarke's face flushed crimson. "What d'you mean?"

"What I say. What really happened to her?"

"She died. You know that. That's why you came to live with us."

Muriel still missed her Uncle Reggie who had died several years ago, ostensibly of heart problems, although she secretly believed her aunt had nagged him to death.

"You said she died in a fall down the stairs. While I was at school," Muriel persisted.

"That's right. A dreadful accident. You know all that."

"Except I don't think that's how she died." Muriel stared at her aunt through narrowed eyes. "I want the truth. I think you owe me that."

When she was typing the Conrad report, she had read over and over again about the renumbering of 44 Cairo Road. The house she had lived in until she was five.

"What happened to my house? Did you ever find out?"

Ida Clarke sipped her tea. It made her sweat. Then she shrugged. "Wasn't it bombed out during the war?"

"You know it wasn't."

"The council must have rented it out again, I suppose. I never went back there. Too many bad memories." She was very looking uncomfortable. "Anyway, why are you asking me this after all this time? The past is the past. Didn't we give you a good home?"

"I'm not saying that, auntie." It always sounded strange, calling her 'auntie'. She wasn't anyone's idea of an 'auntie'. 'Aunt' would have covered it quite adequately.

Muriel could see her start to squirm now. She knew there was something Ida Clarke had never told her. She had always known something about her past wasn't quite right. Sometimes she had caught her aunt and uncle in mid-conversation and look sheepish, obviously changing the subject when she walked in on them. Whisperings and strange looks from friends and neighbours; she had grown up with many of those. Now she needed to know why.

"Then what are you saying?"

Muriel had continued to read the Conrad report. Once she had seen the road and house number in it, she had stopped typing it. She had to find out more. And she had. Much more. Turning over the pages quickly, she soon came to the bit about a woman hanging herself in that very house. *Her* house. Her mother had died in November 1939, which was the date mentioned in Barney's report. Suicide! It had been suicide. Somehow, she had always known it.

She couldn't remember too much about her little brother who had died of diphtheria. All she could remember was how her mother had been inconsolable afterwards and how often she forgot to feed her. She'd always believed what she had been told about her mother's death. It had all made sense to her. The poor woman had been so grief-stricken, she had taken to drink and fallen down the stairs in a drunken stupor. Now she had discovered it had been suicide all along, and a particularly violent one at that.

She now began to wonder about her father. He had died two years before her mother in a tragic building site accident when some scaffolding had collapsed on him. Maybe that had been a lie too.

Things had worked out well enough, however, despite her early orphan status, and she'd little to complain of after she went to live with her aunt and uncle, especially as her meals were always regular now, as well as nourishing. Even during the war years.

"Please, auntie, tell me the truth. I need to know."

Ida Clarke stood up and went to the larder. "Would you like a biscuit?" she asked.

37

Muriel had a lot to think about the next day on her way to work on the bus. She had long given up the tube to the smelly, sweaty crowds, although she had to admit the bus was hardly any better. The smelly, sweaty crowds were on there too, strap hanging above her and giving her the full benefit of their underarm odours. Would this summer never end?

Her aunt had told her very little, despite being asked, then begged, to do so. Muriel knew that deception had been practiced on her, and now she couldn't tell the truth from the lies. She knew, just by the guilty, shifty look on her aunt's face that things she had been told were very far from the true facts. But getting her to admit that had proved impossible.

She sighed as she looked out of the window. People were slogging their way along, most of them obviously fed up with the eternal heat wave. The bus was crawling over Blackfriars Bridge now and she prepared to get off. A man, who had been seated opposite to her, got up at the same time. He smiled as he stood to let her pass. She vaguely took him in; handsome in a boyish way, with a sprinkling of freckles across his nose. Just like Audie Murphy, a film star she was particularly fond of. There was something vaguely familiar about him, too, but she couldn't think why. She was sure she'd never met him before.

Barney was already at his desk when she arrived. "Hi, Barney," she greeted him. He looked up as she came in and smiled at her. Then she remembered Jim. "Er – how's Mr Carmichael?" She nearly called him 'Jim' but remembered the office protocol in time.

"He's – he's very ill, Muriel," said Barney, switching off his smile instantly, almost as if he had been reminded of his brother's condition at the last minute. His mind had obviously been elsewhere.

"Oh, I'm sorry. Will – will he make it, do you think?"

Barney shrugged. "No idea. The doctors aren't committing themselves."

"They never do," said Muriel, seeming to know all about the machinations of the NHS. "What's that you're studying so intently?" She proceeded to make the morning coffee.

"Not for me, dear," said Barney. "I've had a lager."

"A lager? At this time in the morning?" Muriel was shocked.

"I couldn't face coffee in this heat."

Muriel made herself a milky Maxwell House and sat down at her desk. "What are those?" she repeated, indicating the press cuttings under Barney's hands.

"Oh, just a couple of articles from the newspaper archives that Jim copied for us. Not sure why, though. He seemed to think they had some bearing on the Conrad case, but I'm blowed if I can see how."

"Can I have a look at them?"

"Be my guest." Barney stood and brought the cuttings over to her. "Terrible tragedies – both of them.

As you can see, they're connected. But not to the Conrads, as far as I can see."

Muriel read them with growing unease. "These are dated August and November 1939," she observed.

"That's right. Jim was told by a neighbour about them. So, we – well Jim actually – thought they might have some bearing on the case."

"Barney, I used to live at 44 Cairo Road," she said quietly. "And that poor woman is my mother – Doreen Baker was my mother's name." She picked up the first cutting. "And this is my brother. He was called Derek."

Barney's mouth opened so wide, he was in danger of swallowing a wasp that was hovering dangerously close to him. "You're joking!" His voice was almost strangulated.

"I wish I was. I've been told lies all my life about what happened to my mother and brother."

"Who by? Your aunt?"

"Yes, that's right. I went to live with her when I was five. After my mother's death. As it says there." She pointed at the second cutting. "I was always told she fell down the stairs. That it was an accident. I never knew she'd hanged herself."

"Oh, you poor thing." Barney went around her desk and patted her chastely on the shoulder. He seemed at a loss.

"I was also told my brother had died of diphtheria. So, for all I know, he might still be alive."

"Yes, that's true. He could be. He'd be about your age now."

"Yes. A bit younger. I'm even beginning to wonder if my dad died in a building site accident like they told me. It happened when I was two."

"Gosh. You poor thing," Barney repeated, obviously unable to find another epithet for her. "You've had lots of tragedy in your life, haven't you?"

"I just can't take it in. I even asked my aunt yesterday to tell me the truth – and she just stuck to her story."

"Which was?"

"That my mum died in a fall and my brother died of diphtheria."

"I bet you feel betrayed, don't you?"

"That's the understatement of the century."

"Mind you, I expect your aunt lied to you to spare you the real details. At only five, you were obviously much too young to know the truth."

"Yes, but I'm not now."

Muriel looked at Barney through tear-filled eyes. The thought of her mother hanging herself in despair was only half the reason. What was really upsetting her was the fact her mother couldn't bear to go on living without her son, never mind leaving her daughter an orphan. She had been vaguely aware of the preference her mother had shown for her brother, but it hadn't dawned on her before just how deep that affection for him went. Obviously, she herself had inspired no maternal love or, at least, not enough to give her mother a reason to go on living after her brother had gone.

"Why don't you go home, Muriel?" said Barney when she had dried her tears and seemed to be preparing to work. "You're in no state to concentrate."

"No, Barney. I'll be all right. It'll take my mind off things. Besides, you've got as much to contend with as me. You'll need me to hold the fort when you visit Mr Carmichael, for a start."

"Visit him? Oh yes. I'd said I'd take Daisy – Mrs Carmichael – to see him later."

"Good. Then you should do that." She paused as she rolled the paper and carbons into the typewriter. "How – how is the other Mrs Carmichael, by the way?"

Barney visibly tensed at the mention of Pearl. "Still much the same," he muttered.

Muriel could see he didn't want to elaborate, so she began to type. Her fingers hit the wrong keys, something she very rarely did, and the letters were jumbled up. Two of the keys were stuck together. Sighing, she fished in her drawer for the Tippex.

"Well, at least you shouldn't go to Maxwell's this evening," said Barney. "You're in no state – "

"I'm fine, Barney. Fine. I *want* to go. Tonight might be the night another murder happens. I *must* be there."

She screwed the lid back on the Tippex and carried on typing. This time her aim was accurate. She needed to concentrate on something other than her own problems. She would have to face them sometime, but not right now.

"Very well, although I don't approve." Barney's voice seemed far away. "I'll pick you up at nine."

"Okay, Barney. Thanks."

The silence was now only broken by the sound of the typewriter and the ping when she got to the end of a line.

Barney picked up Daisy at eleven o'clock and drove her to the hospital. She was gripping a bunch of pink roses picked from her garden earlier that morning.

"Jim's favourite," she said. Barney sniffed them with pleasure. Their aroma filled the small Morris Minor as they drove along.

"Where's Michael today?" he asked as they neared their destination.

"My neighbour's looking after him. She's been very good."

"That's nice."

Daisy was allowed to go straight in to see Jim, while Barney was asked to wait in the relatives' room. He sat down and took out the press cuttings. He reread them several times, now from an entirely different perspective. He felt so sorry for Muriel. What sort of a mother killed herself and left a small daughter? Then he thought about Daisy. Daisy had been going to do that, hadn't she? Until she saw sense, thankfully. How could she have even contemplated leaving her small son?

His thoughts turned to Pearl. He was looking after her to the best of his ability, but she was ungrateful and cantankerous all the time. She seemed to be holding him solely responsible for her accident and making him pay for it every minute of the day.

He was finally allowed in to see Jim, who looked no better than the day before. There were dark rings under his eyes and his cheeks seemed to have sunken in. His hair even looked greyer.

"How are you feeling, Jim?"

"Like I've been hit by a bus and then run over by a ten-ton truck. Thanks for asking."

"Jim, you shouldn't joke like that."

"It's better than moping, isn't it?"

"I suppose so. You must concentrate on getting better though."

"I am. Daisy is going in for – the procedure tomorrow, she's just told me."

"The sooner the better. Get it over with."

"Yes." There seemed little more to say.

The machine beside them beeped into the silence. "Er, I've read those cuttings, Jim," said Barney, breaking it.

"Well, what do you think?"

"I don't know what it tells us about the Conrad case, but I've got a bombshell to tell *you*."

"What's that?"

Barney proceeded to tell him about Muriel. He regretted it almost at once, as Jim seemed even more shocked by the news than he had been himself. It couldn't do his condition any good at all.

"Calm down, Jim, I shouldn't have told you."

"You bloody well should. The sooner I'm out of here, the better."

"Well, just calm down then. Otherwise the only way you'll get out of here will be in a box."

Jim tried a laugh. It was almost successful. "But – haven't you worked out the connection of those cuttings to the Conrad case?"

Barney sighed. "No, Jim, I haven't. What is it?"

Just then, the martinet of a staff nurse from yesterday entered the room. "Now then, that's enough excitement for one day," she said.

Barney drove Daisy home deep in thought. Just what *was* the connection, he wondered. He'd have to wait until tomorrow to find out, unless he worked it out himself before then.

It wasn't exactly a competition between them, but Jim's intellect always seemed to be one step ahead of Barney's. From their earliest schooldays, Jim's reports and exam results had always been better than his.

"It seems that Jim's a little better," said Daisy, breaking into his thoughts.

"Did they tell you that?"

"Yes."

That was something, at least. It looked as if his brother was going to get better. Barney, somewhere deep inside, was angry with Jim for having a heart attack in the first place. He would have been even more angry if he'd died. What would he do without him?

Now, it seemed, he didn't have to. It was just as well, as he needed Jim's superior intellect to solve the

Conrad case. He certainly wasn't going to solve it on his own.

38

Ted Randall was infatuated. Whenever he saw Muriel Bird, he felt the colour rising to his cheeks and a flurry of something in the pit of his stomach. He wasn't fool enough, however, to think she had the same sensations about him. Ted was nothing, if not a realist. Besides, he had no intention of deserting his wife and family. He was very fond of Joanie, anyway. They rubbed along well together, and their marriage, despite the gambling addiction that threatened to ruin it at any moment, was a success, even if it had been one of the shotgun variety. All he knew was, Muriel's appearance every evening was a highlight he looked forward to, only matched by a (rare) win on the horses.

Ted was doubly happy tonight as Mr Moneybags had turned up again shortly after Muriel. He'd pocketed the fifty pounds as usual, but was disappointed to be told this was going to be the last payout. He could expect no more visits and no more money.

He looked at the clock. Only just gone seven. The cleaners were just getting started. It was going to be a long night, but the money was safely in his pocket and he felt lucky. If he didn't manage to pick out a winner or two tonight, he'd be very surprised. The *Racing Post* was ready and waiting, as he boiled the kettle for tea.

When he was comfortable, he opened the paper, pencil poised. 'Last Chance Saloon' was one horse's name. It seemed to jump out at him. Some sort of omen, he thought to himself. He placed a cross beside it. Then he looked at the name of the horse underneath it: 'Bribery and Corruption'. Was this rag trying to tell him something or was it the horses themselves?

His conscience was anything but clear, but what could he do? He had accumulated two hundred and fifty pounds within the space of a few weeks, a sum he would never have earned if he'd worked till he was a hundred. And his wife was easier to live with these days. A ten-pound note did wonders for her temper.

Suddenly, he stood up, folded the paper and finished his tea in one gulp. It wasn't just his conscience pricking him. Those nags in the paper were pointing out the error of his ways. He wasn't bright enough to see that they were one and the same thing. Muriel Bird was up in the offices cleaning. She could be in danger. Even two hundred and fifty quid wasn't enough to make him forget that. Anyway, the money was his now. He wasn't going to give it back, even if he still had it. Ted Randall knew now what he had to do. He turned to the telephone.

Muriel had arrived a few minutes later than usual that evening. Her short journey on foot from the Blackfriars office to the Maxwell's building had been broken by a short stop for refreshment at a café. Her mind was still full of what she had learnt that morning from Barney's press cuttings. All her life she had been lied to.

She sat for a while, watching familiar figures pass by the window on their way home. They were employees of Maxwell's whose faces she had got to know over the last few days, even though she hadn't spoken to any of them. Most of them looked nice and respectable, unlike herself. She couldn't even inspire the love of her own mother. She must be worthless, she concluded.

Then she'd thought about her husband, Terry. At least he loved her, or so he said he did. But she now wondered about that too. If her mother couldn't love her, it stood to reason that no one else could either. True, Terry showed her affection, but usually only when he wanted to have sex with her. She used to call it making love, but 'having sex' was a more accurate way to describe it now. More clinical and factually correct.

It was strange to think that her brother was probably still alive somewhere. If only she knew where. Maybe she'd be able to inspire love in him, although she doubted it. She had never been one to feel sorry for herself, but she was making up for it now. In spades.

But she still had a use. A purpose. To unmask the charlady killer. She'd show them. Finishing her strawberry milkshake, she stepped out into the evening sunshine and headed for the now familiar office block. Her task, apart from the mere detail of nailing a murderer, was to clean the offices on the sixth floor. Better get started, she supposed.

There was that creepy door man, sitting there with his racing paper and packet of Players. She hated the way he stood up, so politely, wishing her a good evening. She had found him bearable at first, and had even sat and chatted, sharing a cup of tea with him.

She'd thought he had a soft spot for her. How stupid can you get? she now told herself. She didn't even deserve the affection of a runt like Ted Randall.

But, there he was, running to call the lift for her as usual. "Hello, Miss Muriel," he said, smiling. The smile only seemed to make him look more sinister to her now.

She should feel sorry for him, she told herself as she thanked him. But then, who was going to feel sorry for her?

39

Inspector Tony Halliday often worked late, being a conscientious copper, not like the young whippersnappers the Yard seemed to be recruiting these days. He'd never achieved the top echelon of police inspectors, mainly because he'd never been able to toe the party line. He couldn't bring himself to suck up to the right people. It just wasn't in him. Added to which, his success rate was pitifully low. He'd caught his fair share of villains in his time, but his recent track record spoke for itself. Getting past it, he supposed.

But, even though he wasn't likely to be thanked for it, he remained at his desk well past the time to knock off. It wasn't entirely due to dedication to duty, although it came into it. It was also his domestic situation. The atmosphere at home, unlike the weather, was decidedly frosty these days.

His wife was continually nagging at him to retire. He wanted to, of course he did. At least he told himself he did, except quite what he'd do all day hadn't really occurred to him. He could take up a hobby, he supposed. Painting? He couldn't even draw a successful stick man. Bowls? God forbid. No, thoughts of retirement were still only thoughts. He had to solve just one more case. He had to prove to everyone that he wasn't the dinosaur they all thought he was and leave behind a legacy for others to follow.

He studied the file on the charlady murders, facetiously nicknamed by some bright spark as 'Ladies

Who Did'. He had to admit it was quite witty, but it didn't make him laugh. He had to catch the blighter who was killing these poor women. He was thankful that whoever it was had confined himself to one office block. Well, so far, anyway. If he started knocking off charladies willy-nilly all over the place, then his job would be much harder. Impossible, even.

He closed the file. All the interviews had yielded precisely nothing. Nobody had seen anything or anyone suspicious, which was suspicious in itself. There had been a glimmer of hope when one of the charwomen had spoken about a polite and friendly young man. He'd hoped to see her again, he'd told her. That man, he had been convinced, was Murray Sherman. But Mrs Jenkins hadn't picked him out at the identity parade. Could she have been lying? Protecting him because he had been nice to her? Silly cow.

There was a knock at his door at this point and Peter Armitage put his head round it.

"You still here?" Halliday grunted. "Well past your bedtime, isn't it?"

Armitage laughed, obviously used to the Inspector's joshing. Halliday liked him for several reasons, the main one being he didn't suck up to those with more authority, and was even rude to them, in a polite sort of way. Most of the big wigs around Scotland Yard lacked a sense of humour and didn't realise when they were being sent up, which was lucky for Armitage. But his luck would run out one day. Halliday had resolved to have a talk with him before he retired, just to make sure his jokes didn't backfire to the detriment of his career prospects. It was the least he could do.

"Yes, I'm still here," smiled Armitage. "As you can see. There's been a phone call, sir."

"Yes, they happen all the time around here. Anything I should know about?"

"I think you'll be interested in this one, sir."

"Out with it then. I'm about to go home." And, as if to illustrate the point, he stood up and made for the coat stand. He started to put on his jacket, which had been bought when he wasn't quite so fat. Consequently, he didn't attempt to button it up.

"Apparently the murderer could be at Maxwell's right this minute."

Halliday was half in, half out of his jacket now. He tore it off quickly and put it back on the stand. "Right now? As we speak?"

"That's right, sir. This man on the phone said he thought it was possible he was there right now."

"Who was he? The man on the phone, I mean."

"Wouldn't give his name, sir."

"Then what makes him think the killer's there now?"

Armitage shrugged. "Search me. But I thought you should be told, sir."

"Probably a practical joker. How many have we had this week?"

"About six hoax calls and five confessions, sir."

Halliday wasn't particularly hopeful that this call was the one he'd been waiting for, but he felt a tingle of excitement all the same.

"Okay. So why bring this to my attention? Can't you deal with it?"

"Yes, sir. I will if you like. It's just that, well, I think I recognised his voice, sir."

"I see. Who d'you think it was?"

"That night porter. Randall. You remember, sir. You said he seemed a bit shifty when we interviewed him."

"Oh, yes. That surly bugger. I can't believe a concern as big as Maxwell's only employs one security man on nights. Especially not one like him. Didn't look much cop in a fight, did he? Skins would stay on rice puddings with him around, eh?"

Armitage laughed. "Yes, sir. Anyway, you remember you got fed up with him and left me to finish the interview."

"Yes. I could see we weren't getting anywhere with him. All he kept saying was he couldn't be everywhere. Didn't have eyes in the back of his head. Might not have had eyes in the back of his head but he certainly talked out the back of it. I read your report afterwards. There wasn't anything he could tell us, was there?"

"No, sir. But it's always puzzled me how he's never seen anyone suspicious, being on the front desk from six in the evening. Surely, he'd have seen someone or something out of the ordinary?"

Halliday sighed. "He's got his racing paper and his fags. That's all he cares about. You can see it a mile off. I told the personnel manageress when the first murder happened she should get rid of him, or at least step up the security staff. Doesn't seem she took any notice, does it? You'd think she'd have done something about it after the other murders, wouldn't you?"

"Yes, sir. She was a bit of a – er …."

"You were saying?"

"Well, you know. A bit of a …"

"Old trout is the phrase you're searching for, Armitage. Anyway, getting back to Randall. You think this phone call was from him?"

"Could be, sir."

"Then why didn't he say so?"

"Seemed a bit nervous, sir. I reckon he's the type who doesn't like to get involved with the police. Bit dodgy, if you ask me."

"Probably. Still, we'd better take this call seriously. Better call for back up."

"Right you are, sir."

Halliday put on his jacket once more, muttering under his breath. His nerves were like cheese wires.

"This could be it," he told himself. "I've got a feeling in my water. This could really be it. Better get my skates on."

40

She paused in her mopping. It's too hot for this sort of work, she thought. She must have been mad to volunteer for it. But then, what else was she fit for? If ever a woman was sorry for herself, that woman was Muriel Bird.

She supposed she could always skimp her work, seeing as how she was really there to catch a murderer, not to sweep floors or dust desks. But then, if she skimped and was found out, she'd get the sack and the murderer would never be caught. She wrung out the mop with renewed vigour. It was a sorry apology for a mop, though, with half its head missing. Someone should have requisitioned a new one a long time ago, she thought crossly. How could anyone do a good job with equipment like this? "A bad workman blames his tools" she could hear her aunt say. Sod off, aunt, she said under her breath. It would be the last time she'd ever say anything to her, ever again.

She would never forgive her Aunt Ida for withholding the truth about her mother and brother from her. Barefaced lies. How could she have told her her brother had died, when in fact she didn't know where the hell he was? She splashed more water on the floor as she thought these thoughts. The inadequate mop just wasn't up to the task it was made for. Her brow was beaded with sweat and she wiped it away with the back of her hand.

As she pushed the mop along the corridor, she became aware of a rustling noise from behind one of the office doors. Someone was still there but it didn't worry her unduly. Quite a few of Maxwell's employees worked late so there was no need for her to be especially careful. Anyway, if he was the killer, he would have heard her splashing and cursing by now and she would no doubt be his next victim in a very few minutes. She didn't particularly relish the idea, but she supposed it served her right. If she ended up with her head in her water bucket, no one would really care, anyway.

She remained rooted to the spot, waiting for the inevitable to happen. When nothing did, she ventured a tap on the door.

"Er – who is it?" said a voice. A gentle, transatlantic voice. She liked it at once. No one with a voice like that could commit murder. She opened the door and looked in.

"I've come to clean the office," she said, resisting the temptation of saying "can I do you now sir" like Mrs Mopp on the 'ITMA' comedy programmes she'd loved while growing up.

"Oh, that's okay. Come in."

The young man she saw sitting at his desk looked vaguely familiar. He was handsome in a boyish sort of way and he had a freckled nose. Oh yes, she remembered. He'd been on the bus that morning. She had liked him then and, somehow, she liked him even more now. And, what was it about him? Where had she seen him before? Before the bus, even.

"I can come back later if you're busy," she said cheerily.

"Oh no, that's just fine. I'm all through here." He stood up and moved around the desk towards her. He had a buff folder in his hand.

"Thank you," replied Muriel, giving him a smile.

"You're welcome," he said, returning it. "What's a nice girl like you doing in a place like this? I can see you're not cut out for this kind of work."

Even though she always made herself as drab as possible to avoid looking out of place, there was no hiding her intrinsic beauty. Especially not from the likes of Leon Conrad.

She tried not to seem like she was purring. Her reply was brusque if not heart felt. "You mind your manners," she snapped. She hoped he didn't interpret the flush on her face as a flush of pleasure.

"Hey! I didn't mean to give offence. I just think you look charming, that's all. Not like the others."

She didn't reply but her hand went instinctively to her turban. Was it on straight? Did she really look okay? It seemed at least someone appreciated her, which was a big plus in her life at that moment.

He continued to smile at her. "Anyways, I'm just off to see one of your colleagues before I go."

"Oh? Who's that?"

"Mrs Jenkins. Nice lady."

"Freda?"

"Yeah, that's her, I guess." He still had the folder in his hand and she noticed he was trying to conceal the writing on it.

Muriel had passed the time of day with Freda Jenkins on several occasions, being one of the women who had been working at Maxwell's with her mother all those years ago. Freda had told her she had been a special friend of Doreen Baker. But there was something about Freda Muriel didn't quite like, although she couldn't say exactly what.

"Your mum was an angel, darling," Freda had said when she found out who Muriel was. "I cried for days when she – er, died."

Freda Jenkins. So, this young man knew her? Muriel wondered what the relationship could be between a handsome yank and a plain old Mrs Mopp.

"So, you know her then?" Muriel said irrelevantly, all the while trying to see the name on the folder. For some reason, she knew she had to see it. He was hiding it, so that was suspicious for a start. Every nerve in her body was suddenly jangling.

"I've seen her about the place, yeah. Had a nice chat with her a while back. Said I'd look her up next time I worked late. Do you know what floor she's on tonight?"

"Er, the seventh, I think. The top floor."

"Great. No need to take the elevator for one floor."

Before she could say anything else to him, he had sprinted down the corridor and out through the double doors to the stairs.

Suddenly, she knew. She had tried to ignore the nagging voice in her head while they were talking. "This is him" it had been saying. This was the man who was killing the charwomen, and she wished with all her heart it wasn't. She'd got him. But she didn't feel triumphant.

41

Barney was allowed in to see Jim with Daisy this evening. The matron had greeted them with smiles. The rigid staff nurse they had met on the past two occasions had been noticeable by her absence. Off duty tonight, Barney thought. Thank goodness. This one was a much nicer individual.

"Mrs Carmichael? Mr Carmichael?" The matron had come into the waiting room and shaken them both by the hand. At first, Barney feared it was a prelude to bad news, but then he saw the smile on her face.

"Yes – er, I'm his brother, Barney. And this is his wife, Daisy."

"Well, I'm delighted to be able to tell you both that Mr Carmichael is making excellent progress. It seems he's been fooling us all. He's not as ill as we thought."

"Do you mean he hasn't had a heart attack?" asked Daisy eagerly.

"Oh no, Mrs Carmichael. He definitely had a heart attack, but it wasn't as severe as we at first suspected. In fact, he should be fit enough to go home in a few days. The doctor is very pleased with him."

So, a few minutes later, Barney and Daisy were sitting with Jim, who was sitting up and grinning downing grapes for all he was worth.

"Hello, you two," he said.

Daisy bent to kiss him and Barney grabbed his outstretched hand. "I'm so relieved, Jim. You gave us such a scare. Don't ever do it again," said Barney, helping himself to a large handful of Jim's grapes.

"I'll try not to," said Jim happily. "Here, leave me some," he said, snatching the grapes from his brother. "These'll have to do me till tomorrow. The hospital grub is dreadful."

"I'll bring you some food, Jim," said Daisy, stroking his hair. "What would you like?"

"Some of your steak and kidney pud wouldn't go amiss."

"It shall be done. I'll make it tonight and get Barney to bring it to you tomorrow."

"Thanks, love. Anyway, how's things?" Jim looked serious now. He squeezed Daisy's hand as he looked steadily into her eyes.

"I'm going in tomorrow morning, dear," she said. "They're going to sterilize me while they're about it."

"I see."

Barney felt a little uncomfortable at the change in mood. This gynaecological conversation wasn't for his ears. He discreetly moved away from the bed and stared out of the window.

"It's all right," continued Daisy, smiling at Barney's back. "I'm resigned to it now. The most important people in my life are you and Michael. Don't ever scare me like that again."

"And don't you ever scare *me* like that again, either," said Jim, still serious. "I'm sorry you can't have any more children, though."

"So am I. Although before I got pregnant, I'd never thought about having another child. I suppose it's brought it home to me that I would have quite liked this baby to be born."

Tears were standing in her eyes now.

"We could always adopt, you know," said Jim. "I wouldn't mind being a father again. And it'd be company for Michael."

"We'll think about it." Daisy patted his hand and turned to Barney. "It's okay, Barney. You can come back now." She laughed.

Barney coughed with embarrassment. "I didn't want to intrude on your private moment," he said.

"You'd never intrude, Barney. Well, you do know all about it, anyway, don't you?" said Daisy. "And, after all, this baby – er, foetus – would have been your niece or nephew."

Barney hadn't thought of that. It made him sad.

"Anyway, Barney, how's things at the office? Any further on with the Conrad business?" said Jim, looking a little tired now. He sat back on his pillows, holding what was left of the grapes.

Daisy removed them carefully and plumped up his pillows. "I think we'll leave that conversation for another time, love," she said with determination. "You must get some rest now."

"Okay. But just tell me the latest before you go, Barney."

"Nothing to tell, Jim."

"You haven't worked it out, then?"

"How do you mean?"

"Yes. What connects the abduction of the little boy, the mother hanging herself afterwards and Leon Conrad, the man we're supposed to find?"

"Er, no, Jim, I haven't. I've not been giving it my full attention. After what Muriel told me, I just got upset for her."

"How is she?"

"Oh, you know Muriel." Barney thought about the feisty young woman who wanted to be Simone Templar or Samantha Spade. He couldn't help admiring her spirit. Most women were content to type away all day and cook suppers for their husbands at night. Not Muriel Bird, it would seem.

"Yes, I do, and I'm concerned for her," said Jim.

"I shouldn't have told you. You just concentrate on getting well."

"Is she at Maxwell's this evening?"

"Yes. I tried to dissuade her, but she would insist on going. I'll be picking her up in half an hour."

"Good. Make sure you do. I have a feeling she'll be needing you tonight."

With that, Jim closed his eyes and began to snore gently.

42

What would be quicker – lift or stairs? Better not take the stairs, she thought, he might hear me and push me down them.

Muriel pressed the lift's 'up' button and waited for what seemed like an eternity for it to arrive. She was much too late, of course. He would have been there for at least five minutes, time enough to do away with a defenceless old woman.

The lift finally got her to her destination, and she ran along the seventh-floor corridor, heart thumping in her chest and throat. There was a light in one of the offices at the far end. She paused as she reached it, keeping firmly against the corridor wall. The door was ajar. She could hear voices. She could hear *his* voice. Then old Freda's cackle reached her ears. So far, so good then. Still in the land of the living. He must be telling her a joke, letting her have a last laugh before dispatching her.

Gulping down her fear, she pushed open the door, trying to catch her breath at the same time. The young man and old woman looked at her in surprise.

"'Allo, Muriel," said Freda. "What you doing 'ere? I'm doing this floor tonight."

"Er, just wanted a quick word, love." Muriel strived to keep her tone neutral.

"Can't it wait? Me and this young man 'ere are 'aving a pleasant little chat."

"No, Freda, it can't wait. Come here – now!"

"Who are you to give me orders, missy? You're just like your bleedin' mother. She was always throwing 'er weight about like she owned the place."

So, thought Muriel, the truth at last. No wonder her mother killed herself if someone like Freda Jenkins was her 'best friend'.

"Just come here, please. It's important."

All this while, the mysterious young man stood by and waited. He looked annoyed, but not particularly dangerous.

"I ain't taking no orders from you. Can't bear it that I got myself a nice friend 'ere, can yer?" She turned to the man concerned and gave him what she obviously thought was a winning, even beguiling, smile. The smile wasn't returned, but she didn't appear to notice. She even touched her hair in a flirtatious manner.

What did the silly old cow think this man wanted with her? wondered Muriel. It was almost funny if it wasn't so serious. How could she possibly think he fancied her?

"I just need to see you about something," Muriel tried again.

"Your mother was a bad lot," said Freda now, coming towards her, mop in hand. "Left your little brother to be kidnapped by God knows who. We told 'er she weren't fit to be a mother."

Muriel felt like crying: crying for her dead mother, for her lost brother, even for her misguided aunt, who had lost a sister and a nephew. Maybe Barney had been right. Aunt Ida had lied to her for her own good, to spare her feelings. Most people would probably do the same. Maybe she should cut her some slack. It couldn't have been easy for her all these years.

People could be so cruel. Her mother had suffered the loss of her favourite child and, instead of sympathy, had got hounded out of her very existence by this woman and probably the others she'd worked with. She could see them now. All righteous indignation at her poor mother for taking her eye off her child for just a moment. A moment which had proved fatal. But it could have happened to any of them. She remembered her Sunday bible classes suddenly. *Let those without sin cast the first stone.* Hypocrites, the lot of them.

Without any more cajoling, she took hold of Freda by her sleeve and yanked her out of the office, slamming it shut after them.

"'Ere, you let go of me!" protested poor Freda.

"Don't you know you're in danger?" Muriel hissed. "That man is a murderer – *the* murderer! Or had you forgotten what happened to the others?"

"Don't be so daft," said Freda. "'E ain't no murderer, he's a nice young man. Comes all the way from New York, you know. Likes us English 'gals' 'e says."

"Likes killing them, more like."

"Just let me go. You interrupted our conversation. I was telling 'im all about myself. 'E was interested in me."

"I bet he was." Muriel thought for a moment. "Probably wanted to make sure you were worth killing."

This seemed to hit home. "'Ere, you ain't really serious, are yer?"

"What do you think?"

"'E was gonna kill me? Like the others?" The possibility seemed to be sinking in at last.

"I think so. He probably buttered them up like he's buttering you up now before he did what he did to them. You don't really believe he likes you, do you?"

"I thought 'e did."

She looked so tragic now that Muriel suddenly felt sorry for her. Couldn't be much fun being old and unattractive. She could understand how poor Freda would relish being chatted up by such a handsome man. That's how the other three got drawn in, she supposed. At least they went out with a smile on their faces, she thought grimly.

"I'm sorry, Freda. But I think I may have saved your life."

Muriel put the old woman in the lift and pressed the button for the basement. There was no resistance in her now. It was as if all the air had been sucked out of her. She even looked thinner somehow.

"Get yourself a cup of tea and put your feet up," she instructed.

"There you go, giving me orders again." But her protest this time was half-hearted at best. "But maybe you're right. I need a cuppa. I've got some gin to put in it as well."

"That's good," smiled Muriel. "Could do with that myself."

As the door closed, Freda smiled. "Suppose I owe you one. You be careful, now."

Muriel turned back from the lift and walked slowly towards the office at the end of the corridor. Behind that door lurked a killer, she was now quite sure, but she wasn't going to flinch from doing what she had set out to do. Now, more than ever, she had to prove herself. Prove she wasn't the worthless individual everyone thought she was.

But, she thought, should she really risk her life like this? She wasn't the only one she had to think about now. Perhaps it would be better to go down to Ted and get him to call the police. Wait with him there, till they arrived. No, she thought with determination, that would give him time to get away.

She paused outside the office door which was open again. It was if he was expecting her to return, unless he'd got away. But no. She could hear vague rustlings and shufflings inside. He was still there. Here goes then, she said to herself.

43

Two squad cars pulled up with a screech outside the Maxwell's building. It was nearly quarter to nine in the evening and the area was quiet and fairly empty. Night birds had deserted the City for the brighter lights of the West End, which was all well and good, in Tony Halliday's view. Not so many gawpers to contend with.

He instructed his back-up team to await instructions before racing up the front steps and pushing open the heavy double doors. He moved fast for such a heavy man. Sergeant Armitage was on his heels.

Halliday stared at Ted Randall who seemed to shrink behind his desk at the sight of the two policemen.

"Now, then, Randall. Did you call us just now?"

"Me? Er – no. Not me. What seems to be the trouble?"

"Don't play games with me," said Halliday in his most threatening tone. "Sergeant Armitage, here, recognised your voice."

"Er, no. Well…"

"Come on. Why deny it? You were just doing your good citizen duty. Unless of course this is a wild goose chase? And let me tell you now, if it is, I don't reckon your chances of going home tonight."

Randall sighed. "I just don't want to get involved, that's all. But that poor girl – I couldn't let 'er go up there with 'im on the premises."

Halliday drummed the reception desk with impatience. "Are you telling me there's someone up there with the man now? The man you suspect is the killer?"

"She's only a young girl," said Ted.

"A young girl?" Was this fiend starting on the younger ones, now? he wondered.

"Yeah, I don't want 'er to get 'urt."

"So, let me get this straight," said Halliday, giving Ted a glare that told him he was on a very sticky wicket indeed. "You called the Yard. Right?"

"I dialled nine-nine-nine. Yeah, I did."

"So, you know there's someone here who could be the killer we're after?"

"Er, yeah. I wouldn't 'ave called you otherwise."

"And in all this time, this is the first occasion you've ever seen a suspicious character enter the building?"

Ted Randall seemed to be trying to formulate a reply to this.

"Because, if you're telling me you made no attempt to stop him before this, that's a very serious matter indeed. And now I presume he's got the run of the place? No other security staff here, I take it?" He paused but didn't wait for Ted to reply. "No, I know the security in this place is lamentably poor. There'll be questions later. And I'll certainly be talking to *you* later, Randall. So, don't even think about going anywhere."

"I ain't off duty till six," Ted informed him.

Halliday was sure now that Randall knew exactly who the killer was. He'd take a bet this horrid little man had been bribed to keep quiet, and he'd probably only called tonight because he was worried about a young woman who was also on the premises. Probably had taken a fancy to her and was doing his Sir Galahad bit. A little too late for the three old dears who'd ended up with their heads in their own buckets, of course. But he obviously didn't care about them.

Halliday turned to Armitage. "You'd better stay with our friend here." He looked at Randall again. "Any idea which floor we need to head for?"

Randall shrugged. "No."

"If it's not too much trouble, can you at least tell me how many floors there are in this bloody place?"

"Seven."

"Right. Can you alert the others, Armitage? We've got six men, with me that's seven. We'll take a floor each."

Randall, under the watchful eye of Sergeant Armitage, did his best to look innocent, but it wasn't a success. His whole body language left Armitage in no doubt here was a man who knew he was in trouble. Serious trouble.

"I ain't never clapped eyes on that man till tonight. I swear." His voice was a whine that made the police sergeant inwardly squirm. Like the screech of chalk on a blackboard.

"I never said you did," said Armitage, blandly.

Randall wasn't a stupid man. Far from it. He had protested too much. He should have waited until they'd accused him. He had dug himself into a hole that he knew he'd have the devil of a job getting out of.

"Would you like a cup of tea, sergeant?" he tried.

45

Muriel peeked round the office door. She couldn't see any harm in him as he stood in the middle of the room, hands in pockets. She must have made a mistake. This couldn't possibly be the man who'd terrorized three old ladies out of their very existence. No one could look that casual with murder on their mind.

"Come in, why don't you?" Muriel realized she'd given her presence away. He had seen the tip of her shoe in the doorway. "I know you're there."

Muriel slowly followed the tip of her shoe with the rest of her. She tried to square up to him, but being only a little over five feet two inches, she was no match for his six feet one inch. Her bravado still hadn't deserted her, however, and she stood her ground.

"What are you doing here?" she said. "Are you an employee of this company? I've never seen you before."

"I guess you wouldn't have," said Leon, smiling. "I'm not, shall we say, on the official personnel records of this place. But I've been here before as you've probably sussed by now."

This sounded ominous. She cleared her throat. "So how did you get past Ted? I presume you don't have a legitimate reason for being here."

Leon sat on the desk and leaned back, arms folded, looking intently at her. There was something in his eyes that she couldn't quite read. It seemed almost like a recognition. It was something she was feeling too.

This man was something to her, something more than just a man she'd seen on the bus, who'd smiled at her. Something much more. Then a thought struck her. The man in the photograph: Leon Conrad.

"Easy. Men like him don't need much persuading. Show them the dough, that's all they care about."

"You bribed him?"

He gave her an enigmatic smile. "Natch. Like giving sweets to a baby. Tell me," he said softly. "What was your mom's name?"

This was certainly not a question she expected. "My mom – er, mother? What's that got to do with you?"

"Pretty much everything. Please – please tell me."

There was no threat, just a pleading look.

"Not that it's any of your business, but her name was Doreen Baker."

"I knew it. Do you remember your little brother?"

"My brother? How on earth did you know I had a brother?"

"So, you did. Do you remember him at all?"

"No, hardly at all. He – he got abducted when he was four and I was only ten months older. I've never seen him since. I actually thought he'd died. I was told he'd died of diphtheria."

"Well, I can tell you he didn't die. He's still very much alive."

"How – how do you know?" Although she knew.

"Because that's me. I'm your brother."

"But – how did you know? What made you ask?" It was too much to take in. Her legs were wobbly and she felt herself begin to tune out. His face and the office desk were going round and round.

"I heard what that woman said – about your mom. About how they'd all made her life a misery after she'd lost me. They drove her to suicide. The evil bitches."

"But – but …."

"Here – you'd better sit down before you fall down," he said as she began to sway dangerously. He placed her carefully in a chair. He drew off some water from the cooler immediately outside in the corridor and gave it to her.

"Drink this," he said, his voice as soft and melty as velvet.

She drank greedily, all the while trying to focus on him. She felt a little better after a few moments and things came back to normal around her. Except they weren't normal anymore. She'd just met a brother who'd long been dead to her.

"So - so where have you been all this time? Who took you? How did you find me? Why are you here, of all places?"

"Hey, one thing at a time," he smiled. "I know it's a shock. I was reared by an American woman and her chauffeur. Nice guy that Bill. Nicer than her."

"You're not making a lot of sense. Bill? Who's Bill?"

"I just told you. The chauffeur. But he was more than that to her. And to me."

"Her? Who's her?" Muriel's grammar had completely deserted her.

"The woman who had me abducted. Rolling in dough, but she'd no time for me. Left it all to Bill. I'll never understand why she wanted me in the first place."

"She must be very selfish – very wicked. She took you and made my mother kill herself."

"Yeah, well, we can't blame Jeanne – not entirely, anyways."

"Jeanne?"

"That's the woman I've been calling 'mother' all these years."

"Oh, right. But who else is to blame? It was because she took you that my mother killed herself."

"Yeah, sure. I've a score to settle with her, too. But it was these women here that did it," he said. There was malevolence in his eyes now.

Muriel was puzzled for a moment, then she remembered what Freda had said to her only a few moments before. "Oh, you mean they blamed her for letting you out of her sight?"

"Yeah – well, I guess that's what happened. I have to blame them – there's no one else left."

"So, you've lived in the States all this while, then?"

"Sure."

"No wonder you were never found."

He gave her an appraising look. "What I don't get is, why would your – *our* – mom kill herself when she still had you?"

"She never really cared so much about me," said Muriel, feeling sorry for herself once again. "You were always her favourite."

"I guess that's something I can't change."

"*Nothing* can be changed. The past is the past. But it's wonderful. I've got you back. Derek."

"Yeah, Derek. What a God awful name."

"Are you – are you called something else, then?" Although she knew.

"Leon."

"Leon. Nice. Like a lion."

"Yeah, I'll give Jeanne her due. She gave me a decent name. Said I looked like a lion with my colouring and all."

"I like your colouring – especially your freckles." Muriel was smiling at him now.

"Darn it, I hate my freckles." He put his hand over his nose as if to shield them from her view.

"But they're charming," insisted Muriel.

"Do you really think so?"

"I do. Just like Audie Murphy."

They sat looking at each other in silence for a few minutes, drinking each other in. Then he spoke.

"You're beautiful, you know that? What's your name?"

"Muriel."

"Are you married? I bet you are, a doll like you."

"Yes. I am."

"Lucky guy."

"But what are you doing here? Did you know there've been some awful things happening in this building? Three charwomen have been murdered."

He said nothing, but a sardonic grin began to spread across his handsome features.

"You'll laugh at this, but I thought *you* were the killer," said Muriel. "That's why I got Freda out of here. I thought she was going to be your next victim."

"She was."

The room began spinning around again. Her long lost brother now found. Her long lost brother with the lion's name. Her long lost brother a cold-blooded killer. Her long lost brother who Barney and Jim had been looking for.

"Here, drink this," he was saying. He'd removed a hip flask from his trouser pocket and was pushing the nozzle into her mouth. The sudden rush of bitter alcohol hit her like a ten-ton truck.

"You – you're not serious! But – but – but – why?" She coughed, pushing the flask away. That was enough of that. She needed to think straight.

"'Cos I gotta do it. I found out who they were. Who were left here that used to work with our mom. They were responsible for killing her. I have to avenge her. I gotta, don't you see? For all the life I lost and can't get back. My real mom who loved me and I never knew her. I had to – I needed to do it. Don't you see?"

"No. I don't. You can't kill people and expect to get away with it, no matter how bad you think they are or how justified you think you are in doing it. You'll have to pay for it." She paused. The full import of what she was about to say was shocking to her. "With your life."

He seemed unperturbed, however. "Nah, I'll just go back to the States. They won't get me there."

"You can't do that. What about me? I can't just let you walk out of my life now that I've found you. Now that we've found each other."

"Come with me, then." He said it as if he meant it.

"I can't. How can I? What about my husband?"

"Gee. I wish I'd found you sooner. Before I – before all this. Before I messed up. You got kids, Muriel?"

She shook her head. She couldn't speak. The tears were falling unchecked and the back of her throat ached with the effort of trying to stop them.

He put his arms around her and she surrendered to him. They were like lovers. She pulled away quickly. It wouldn't help matters if incest were added to his other crimes.

Then they heard the lift. "Who's that?" he said quickly.

"Just one of the cleaners, I expect."

But the noise didn't involve the clanking of pails. The heavy footfalls were unmistakable. Police size elevens. Leon grabbed her and they both hid under the desk. They could see the copper's feet from their vantage point.

"No one here, guv. The light must have been left on by the cleaner."

He switched off the light and was gone.

They heard his retreating footsteps with relief.

"Okay," said Leon. "Is there another way outta here?"

"Out of the building, do you mean?"

"Yeah."

"I – I suppose there must be. Fire escape?"

"Hey, how long have you worked here?"

"Not long. I'm not really a cleaner, you know."

"You surprise me. So, you doing this for pin money?"

"Not really, although the extra money comes in useful."

They scrambled out from under the desk.

"So why are you doing it then?"

"To catch the killer, of course. You see, I work for a private detective agency."

He stared at her. This piece of information, unlike the threat of the noose, seemed to give him a jolt. "You're a private dick? You don't look much like one."

She allowed herself a smile. One disguise was enough. She looked like a charwoman and charwomen don't usually go in for private eye work.

"Well, I am," was all she could say.

"Gee! And you've been hired to catch *me*?"

"Well, not *you*. But, as it's turned out, yes. To catch you."

"You gonna hand me over?"

"I – I have to."

"You know I can't let you do that." His tone was serious, even a little threatening now. "Did you call the police? Is that why they're here?"

"No, of course I didn't. I didn't know you were the killer before I met you just now."

"Yeah, I guess so. You better come with me."

Before she could protest, he took her firmly by the hand and pulled her after him along the corridor to the door leading to the stairs. He began climbing, but Muriel dug in her heels and he had to stop.

"Come on!" he hissed. "There's no time for this. The door to the roof must be up there." He yanked her arm. She winced in pain and bit her lip.

"No, Leon, it's not right. You're my brother and I'll do everything I can to help you. But I won't help you escape."

"You don't get to choose," he said, his tone dark. He grabbed her under the arms and threw her over his shoulder. "I'm glad you're a featherweight," he said, climbing quickly the last few steps to the exit door. He put her down, still hanging onto her by the arm, and with his free hand forced open the door to the roof.

He pulled her out after him. The heat of the dying day hit them, as did the flashing lights from the police cars below. He dragged her to the edge of the roof.

"They won't get me while I've got hold of you," he said into her ear. "If I jump, you'll go with me."

"No, Leon! You can't!" She suddenly realized she wanted to live. She wanted very much to live. She wanted Terry and she wanted the new life stirring inside her to live too.

"It's them or me." He slumped down against the safety rail, forcing her down beside him. "We can jump together. We won't have to be parted anymore."

Muriel looked at the stranger beside her. He was her brother, there was no doubt of that. They looked alike, and, even though he spoke with a New York accent, the intonations in his speech were the same.

But she didn't *know* him, and now there was no time left. No time at all.

45

Barney drew up near the Maxwell building at just after nine-thirty. He had to park quite away from its imposing façade as there were two large black saloons in the way. They had give-away lights on them and he was filled with dread. What was happening? Muriel was in there. Was she in danger? Were the police in there saving her and catching the killer?

As he approached the building, his way was barred by a uniformed officer. There seemed to be a proliferation of them now he came to look. And more were arriving. And there was Tony Halliday with a megaphone.

"What's going on, officer?" he asked the uniformed man nearest to him.

"May I ask what your business is in this building, sir?" said the copper, answering his question with a question, in the time-honoured way all coppers had. Barney had never got a straight answer from a law man yet, apart from his mate Tony, of course. What *was* he doing with that megaphone?

"I've come to collect my secretary," he said.

"Is she working late?"

"Yes. That's right. Actually, I'm a bit late myself."

"So, you work here at Maxwell's, sir?"

"No, no. I'm just here to collect my secretary."

The copper looked mystified now. "Er, but if she's your secretary, and she's working in there, then surely you must work in there too?"

"Don't mess about asking stupid questions," said Barney unwisely.

"There's no call to adopt that tone, sir. As you can see, there is a major incident going on here, and I need to know who goes in and out of the building, as well as who is in there at the moment."

"I'm sorry," said Barney, calming down. After all, the plod was only doing his job, he supposed. "But I'm a bit worried. My secretary is in that building and there is a rather large police presence. Is she in danger?"

"Can you tell me who your secretary is, sir?"

"Her name's Muriel Bird, and she works for me. I'm a private detective."

Light seemed to be beginning to dawn on the young officer. "Oh, I see, sir. I think you might have to prepare yourself for a shock."

Barney felt his legs and stomach turn to water. Was he too late? Was she already dead? Another victim of the charlady killer?

"What? Tell me!"

"Is your secretary a young lady, sir? Fair hair, slim."

"That's her. Yes. What's happened to her?"

"If you care to back away sir to across the road where the other sightseers are gathered…" He paused. It was clear he had nothing but contempt for them. "…you should be able to see her. She's on the roof."

"On the roof?" The need for a megaphone was obvious to him now. "Is she – is she threatening to jump off?" Surely not, he thought. There was no one with more *joie de vivre* than Muriel Bird.

"No, sir. But the man with her is."

Tony Halliday came over to them at that moment. "It's all right, officer. I know this man."

"Yes, sir. Very good, sir."

"Tony! Oh God. What's happened?" Why hadn't he got there sooner? He should have been there at nine. But would it have made any difference if he had?

Halliday explained quickly, all the time staring up at the roof. Barney followed his eye line. There she was. She looked in one piece, for the moment at least. The man beside her looked desperate though, and he was holding her by the arm. He watched her struggle.

"Don't Muriel! Don't struggle," he called out to her. "You'll fall!" But he knew she couldn't hear him.

"Can I talk to her with that thing?" he asked Tony.

"No, you can't," was the sharp reply. "What were you thinking, getting your secretary involved in all this?"

"She insisted. I couldn't stop her. Anyway, it looks like she's brought our man out into the open."

Halliday grunted. "And now look at the mess we're in. He's threatening to jump and take her with him."

Barney could see several police officers on the roof now. They were standing well back, however. Frightened to move.

Oh God, thought Barney. If anything happens to that girl, he'd never forgive himself.

Leon Conrad knew he was cornered. He wasn't going to get out of this alive. His sister Muriel was beside him, a sister he never knew he had until a few short weeks ago, but she was frightened to death. The tell-tale trickle now pooling on the ground underneath her skirt was proof of that. What sort of monster had he become?

His mother was dead, and no amount of killing was going to bring her back. He'd taken three lives and there was no way he could undo that. If only he'd found Muriel before he'd begun his crusade. She would have soon persuaded him he was taking the wrong path and he would have happily given up and been content to get to know his big sister. Now he never would.

There were three police officers on the roof, hovering, ready to pounce. But they wouldn't dare while he had Muriel with him.

Suddenly he knew what he must do. "You won't take me alive," he shouted at them.

They moved forward slowly. They were in perfect sync, like a ballroom dance team.

He pulled Muriel to her feet. She was sobbing quietly, seemingly resigned to her fate. He pushed her roughly towards the oncoming coppers and turned quickly. Before anyone could stop him, he had disappeared over the edge of the roof.

46

Barney drove carefully through the dark streets, his thoughts numerous and muddled. But it was clear to him now that Leon Conrad, the man he had been hired to find, was the charlady killer and, even more astonishing, Muriel's brother. The one she had thought dead all these years. Everything had been cleared up in one go. She'd solved the murders and the Conrad case single-handedly.

He watched her now out of the corner of his eye. She was sitting beside him, quite still, dazed and unfocused. Halliday had wanted to interview her straight after her rooftop ordeal and the death of her brother, but Barney had put his foot down.

"Give the girl a break," he had told the Inspector.

"All right. I can see she's in shock," Halliday had granted. "But I shall have to speak to her tomorrow."

Barney felt totally responsible for what had happened, despite Muriel's assurances that she'd been fully prepared for any consequences from her self-imposed adventure. But he knew she was regretting it now.

They were nearing her home, when he ventured to speak to her. "How – how are you, dear?" he said gently, easing the car into a parking space and switching off the engine. He wanted to make sure she was fit to face her husband before he took her to her door a few streets away.

"I'm okay, thanks," she said. It was as if a robot was speaking to him.

"You're definitely not okay. All this is going to be all over the TV and papers. Are you prepared for that? What will your husband say?"

"Oh, I'll make sure Terry understands that I was just in the wrong place at the wrong time. I won't bring you into it. I did it off my own bat." She seemed a little more normal now, as she realized she was nearly home.

"I don't care about that," said Barney, a little untruthfully. He'd never met Terry Bird, but from what she had said about him, he could handle himself well in a fight. "I just want to make sure you're okay. You need to get a good night's sleep."

"I will. Don't worry."

"I wish you'd let them take you to see the police doctor before coming home," he said. "He could have given you a sedative or something. You might need it, you know."

"Oh, don't worry about me," she said. "I just want to get home."

"Are you – are you going to tell Terry about your brother?"

She sat there in silence and Barney began to think she hadn't heard his question. Then she spoke.

"What would be the point? I didn't have a brother yesterday and I haven't got one tonight. It's best left as it is. Will it all come out in the papers?"

"No. I told Inspector Halliday that the press wasn't to be told the details of your relationship to – to that man. And you mustn't talk to any newspaper reporters yourself. They can be very persistent. It's going to be hard for you for the next week or so. Until all the fuss dies down."

"I know. I'm prepared. I'll talk to Inspector Halliday and no one else."

"Good girl. Now, you must take the rest of the week off. And, well, I think we'll need to have a chat when you get back."

"A chat? About what?"

"About your role with the agency."

"Oh, that."

Barney was a little surprised she didn't seem more enthusiastic. Surely, she must suspect he was going to offer her a new role, that of private investigator? No more typing for Muriel Bird. But, he supposed, she was still in shock. Maybe it was too soon to mention it. But he did anyway.

"Now that you've proved yourself, I can't expect you to carry on being just a secretary, can I?"

Muriel looked at him and smiled wearily. "All I ever want to do from now on is be a secretary."

"What? But – well, I thought – I mean, what has tonight been all about, then? Nearly getting yourself killed just to prove you're as good as we are. All right. You proved it. You're *better* than we are. Much better."

A tear was poised to trickle across her nose, and Barney reached for his hanky. She brushed it away before he could do it himself. Poor kid, he thought sadly. What a night she must have had. She's obviously not thinking straight.

"Come on, Muriel. We need you. The agency needs you. We can always get another secretary. Muriel?"

She didn't reply.

"Don't you want to be a private investigator?"

"No. You see I found out I wasn't as brave as I thought I was. And, besides – "

"Yes?"

"I'm going to have a baby."

47

It was gone half-past-ten by the time Barney reached home after dropping Muriel off. He turned the key in the lock and braced himself. He was much later than usual. Even though he had ensured a neighbour looked in on Pearl and cooked her supper, she would be angry. Past angry by now, he thought bitterly. He wished he could have cared that she had been left alone for so long, a poor invalid, wheelchair-bound. But somehow, he couldn't.

It was as he feared. She was sitting there, her knuckles white as she clutched the arms of her chair. Not for the first time, Barney wished there were electrodes attached to it.

"Where've you been till this time of night?" she spat at him.

He didn't feel like answering. Even if he'd told her the truth about the night's events, she wouldn't have been interested. In Pearl's world, the only thing in it that mattered was Pearl.

"Answer me!" she insisted, wheeling her chair towards him. He stepped aside quickly as she threatened to mow him down in the hall where he stood.

"I've had a lot on my plate today, Pearl. I'm sorry. Didn't Mrs Bulstrode come in and see to your evening meal?"

"Yes, no thanks to you." It was a grudging admission.

"No thanks to me? It was me who arranged for her to come in. You could at least be a bit grateful, if not to me, then at least to her."

"Why? Why should I be grateful to you or anyone? I don't think my accident deserves any thanks from me."

"Look, I'm sorry, Pearl. But the accident wasn't my fault. If anyone's to blame it's those two long streaks of misery who put you up to it. I notice they never come and visit you either."

"They're too busy with the new act," she muttered, wheeling backwards to allow him into the sitting room. "They had to find a replacement for me. Anyway, what do you care whether they come and see me or not? I'm not well. I feel sick all the time and you're never here!"

Moan, moan, moan, he thought. Doesn't she ever think about anyone but herself?

"How was your physio yesterday? I forgot to ask."

"And that's another thing. You expect Mrs Bulstrode to do all your dirty work for you, carting me back and forth from the hospital for my appointments."

"Only this once. I took you last week."

"Oh, thanks a lot. Why should I thank you for only doing what any decent husband would do?"

"I do all I can, Pearl. Besides, I spoke to the doctor last week when I was there waiting for you."

"So?" She suddenly looked very shifty.

He wondered what had happened to the beautiful, happy girl he had first met what seemed a lifetime ago. He tried to conjure her up, but failed. "He said there was no physical reason why you shouldn't be able to walk again. He said he could only suppose it's psychological. It's a barrier you have to get over."

"Don't you think I'd walk again if I could?" She hadn't lost her shifty look, however.

"Would you?" Barney wondered if the barrier to her walking again was the fear of losing him. It had crossed his mind more than once.

"What d'*you* think? You try sitting in this chair all day and see how you like it."

"Look, Pearl, why don't you try to stand up? Give me your hands. I'll help you." He stepped towards her, hands outstretched.

"You keep away from me!" she screamed at him. "Don't touch me!"

"All right, Pearl. No need to get so upset. I'm only trying to help."

She was crying now, but he still couldn't have cared less. He was so tired. Physically and mentally. And tomorrow was going to be another difficult day. He was to take Daisy to the hospital for her 'procedure' as she kept calling it now. It didn't seem such a big deal, she said, if she described it as that. 'Abortion' and 'termination' were two words she couldn't bear to utter anymore.

"Come on, Pearl. I've got to lift you up now." He made towards her again.

"You're not going to make me stand up, then?"

"No, of course I'm not. I never want to hurt you, Pearl. I'm just taking you to bed, that's all."

Later that night, he lay awake beside her. Her light snores, which he had once thought sweet, like the snufflings of a sleeping child, now only aggravated him. He knew sleep would elude him for the rest of the night now, and he felt like fetching the kitchen knife and driving it into her heart.

His mind was too active to shut down anyway. He couldn't blame Pearl's snoring entirely, he knew. Poor Muriel. Poor Daisy. And, he added with much reluctance, poor Pearl too. The women in his life were having a hard time of it one way or another.

Then his thoughts turned to Dilys. At least she was all right, he supposed. But he wasn't a man with much imagination. He didn't know the heartbreak she was suffering because they couldn't be together. As he lay there, sleepless, beside his invalid wife, Dilys was crying softly into her pillow, wide awake too.

48

Barney sat at his desk, feeling like the loneliest man in the world. There was no Muriel to make him an unwanted coffee and no Jim to cheer him up with his good-humoured banter. The news was good about his brother, of course, but even though he was being released from the hospital in a day or two, there was no question of him coming back to work right away. The news was also good about Muriel, as she was due to come back to work next week, content to type his letters and reports, make the tea, and nothing else.

He mulled over the conversation he'd had with Muriel the night before. She'd told him as much as she could about her ordeal, although some of her recollections were fuzzy at best. She'd nearly fainted twice she'd told him. No wonder, he thought. She must be a strong-minded person to have survived all that intact. He only wished he'd been there to help, even though he had to admit he'd probably have been more scared than Muriel. So, no help at all, really.

The morning hadn't started well, either. He'd driven Daisy to the hospital but she'd almost chickened out.

"Drive me back," she'd said as he drove the car into the hospital car park. "I can't go through with it!"

It had taken a lot of persuading, and reminding her of what she would be losing if she didn't. "Think of poor Jim," he'd said. "Do you want him to have another heart attack, one that could be fatal this time? Then where would Michael be? No mum or dad to bring him up."

She'd cajoled him. "You'd make a lovely substitute parent. He loves you so much already."

He'd had to remind her of his own situation with Pearl in a wheelchair, moaning her head off day and night. "That's no place for a little boy," he'd said wisely.

It had done the trick in the end. He'd watched her disappear down the corridor with the nurse, calling after that he'd be there when she was ready to come home.

He sat at his desk now, wondering what to do next. There was still a lot of admin to catch up with, but he had no heart for it. He had half a mind to close the office for the day and drown his sorrows in the pub across the road. But that way, he knew, led to ruin. He'd better not get dependent on alcohol, he'd told himself. He had to be strong. Except, why should he be? No one had any sympathy for him. He wanted to be with the woman he loved and couldn't, but nobody seemed to appreciate that.

As he was thinking these maundering thoughts, the door suddenly burst open and Barney looked up to see a strapping six-footer glowering over him.

"Er, can I help you? Do you have an appointment?"

"No, I don't have an appointment." There was no hint of an apology in the man's tone.

"Well, you see, you need to make one. My secretary, unfortunately, is away for a few days, but if you call on Monday, I'm sure she'll be happy to make you one."

"Your secretary is at home – *my* home and I don't need an appointment," said Terry Bird, his fists clenched menacingly.

"Oh, I – I see. You're – you're Terry then, are you?" Barney was sensing danger, quick on the uptake as ever.

"Well done, pal. That's right, I'm Muriel's husband and I don't appreciate you sending my wife up on the roof with killers in the middle of the night."

Barney resisted the temptation to put him right on one or two points. Nine o'clock was hardly the middle of the night, and there had only been one killer to contend with. He didn't say any of this, however, sensing these incidentals wouldn't cut any ice with the man in his present mood.

"I – I'm sorry," Barney began.

"So you ruddy well should be. I ought to knock your ruddy block off. Sending her out after homicidal maniacs! Especially in her condition. She's going to have a baby, you know."

"Yes, she told me last night. If I'd known sooner, none of this would have happened. But I did try to persuade her not to – not to get involved in the investigation, you must believe that. But she has a mind of her own, Mr Bird, as I'm sure you know."

"Don't I know it. The silly cow could have got herself killed. It was your job to stop her." He paused for a moment. "Hang on," he then said, thumping the desk. "She told you she was pregnant last night?"

"Yes. After – after all that had happened. I swear I didn't know before."

"Well, it seems you knew before me. She only told me when you so very kindly dropped her off last night." His tone was beyond sarcastic.

"Er, well, you can hardly blame me for that."

Terry Bird humphed by way of acknowledgement of this reasonable observation.

Barney continued before the young man could think of a suitable retaliation. "Look, I know, I know. You're right. I shouldn't have let her go into that danger. I blame myself entirely. If there's anything I can do – "

"I think you've done enough already, Mr Carmichael," said Terry, obviously calming down a bit. "And I don't want her to come back here ever again. If you just give me the wages she's owed and her P45 – "

"Just a minute," said Barney, feeling decidedly narked now. "Did she say she wanted to leave?"

"No, but I'm telling her. She'll do as I say. I don't want her put in harm's way, not now she's got to think of the baby."

"But she told me she wanted to stay on – " He put up his hand as he saw Terry about to object. "But only as my secretary. She told me that herself."

This seemed to take the wind out of Terry's rather over-inflated sails. "Oh, did she?"

"Yes, so I hope you'll let her carry on here?"

"Well, in that case. All right, if she wants to."

"Thank you, Mr Bird. I appreciate that."

The young man turned to leave, but turned back abruptly. "But the minute I hear she's chasing crooks down dark alleys I'll have your guts for a tennis racquet. Okay?"

"Er – okay."

Barney, relieved to see the back of Terry Bird, poured himself a cold lager from the fridge, all resolutions to steer clear of the demon alcohol in abeyance for the time being. He was feeling decidedly sorry for himself. He just hoped no one else was going to barge in and threaten to punch his lights out.

That hope, however, was dashed by Inspector Tony Halliday who entered the office ten minutes later looking even more dangerous than Terry. Barney could almost see steam coming out of his ears as his Inspector friend paced up and down the office, apparently telling him off for something or other. Barney didn't quite understand what Tony's beef was with him, but he waited in patient silence while the man got whatever it was off his rather expansive, barrel-shaped chest.

"Have you quite finished?" Barney asked as Halliday slumped into the chair opposite him. "You're not doing your blood pressure any good, you know."

"I gave up on that years ago," muttered the Inspector. "What the hell were you thinking, sending that poor girl into danger like that? Are you out of your tiny mind?"

Barney sighed, explaining to the Inspector just as he had to Terry Bird, how he had tried to dissuade her to no avail. Halliday looked at him when he had finished. That look wasn't friendly.

"You're a complete arse," he said. "But I suppose you can't help it."

"Charming! Would you like a lager to cool you down?"

Thankfully, the lager proved an ice-breaker, and Halliday smiled as he enjoyed his first sip of the cold beer. "Just what the doctor ordered," he said. "You do yourself proud here, I must say. The private detective business must be paying well."

"So, so," smiled Barney, glad to have his friend back on side. It was surprising what a cold lager could do where all supplications, apologies and excuses failed.

"I still think you should have made more of an effort to stop her," said Halliday.

"I don't know why you're complaining. She got your man for you, didn't she? She solved your case for you."

"Hmph! I'd rather we'd taken him alive, though."

Barney had no come back for this. Secretly, he was glad the man has escaped the hangman's noose. For Muriel's sake, especially.

"How long had she been posing as a cleaner at Maxwell's, Barney?"

"Oh, not long," said Barney, vaguely. "I told her every time she shouldn't go."

"It was just as well that night porter took a shine to her," observed the Inspector, draining his lager can. "It prompted him to alert the Yard. I suppose we should thank her for that – for being, as it were, a pretty girl. A damsel in distress, you might say, appealing to Randall's better nature. Looking at him, though, you wouldn't have thought he'd got one."

"He obviously knew the killer was there, then?"

"Of course, he knew. And he'd known all the times before, you can bet your bottom dollar. The only trouble will be proving it."

"Well, that's where I can help you," smiled Barney. "Muriel told me, amongst other things last night, that Leon Conrad had been bribing him."

"You mean to tell me that bastard knew who the murderer was from day one and he never said anything about it?"

"That's right. Apparently, the money was too good to pass up."

"The evil little sod. I'll throw the book at him." Halliday was in a much sunnier mood than when he had first arrived. "Accessory before and after the fact. That's worth hundreds of years in prison, that is."

"Oh, hundreds!" laughed Barney. "At the very least."

49

Dilys Amory felt she needed a new hat. She didn't think women were wearing hats so much these days, at least not the younger ones, but she never felt completely dressed going out without one. She had quite a selection of hats already, most of them had been bought for her by her soon to be ex-husband. But she didn't want to wear any of those anymore. She didn't want any reminder of what had been, when she and Brian had been very much in love. In those days, nothing could have kept them apart.

But things changed, nothing ever stayed the same. She'd had to accept it. Brian Amory had met a younger woman, and no doubt he was buying *her* hats now. Of course, reasoned Dilys, if she was younger than herself she probably didn't wear them, He'd have to buy her jewelry instead, or a fur coat. Serve him right if she cost him the earth. Dilys had been perfectly content with a two-guinea hat. That'd show him what he was missing.

She had spent a restless night, dreaming about Barney Carmichael. If only he were free. She had to renounce him when Pearl had her accident, it had been the only honourable thing to do. And Barney himself couldn't, in all conscience, leave his wife in the lurch, now that she needed him most. It couldn't be done. So, a new hat was the only thing.

She rode to Oxford Street on the number 139 bus, enjoying the longish journey, wrapped in her thoughts. The sun was still as hot as ever and, as she was sitting next to the window, she soon realized she'd have to move away if she wasn't going to expire from heatstroke. Luckily, a man got off at that moment and she was able to nab his seat in the shade before anyone else did. The continued heatwave was probably playing havoc with the harvest, she thought, and gardeners must be despairing. Only this morning, she'd heard on the news that there was a threat of putting standpipes in the streets if it didn't rain soon.

It was just after eleven o'clock when she entered Debenham's. The overwhelming smell of expensive perfumes that assailed her nostrils was too much for her. She started to cough. She passed quickly through the department, ignoring various salesgirls' attempts to interest her in new brands all the way from Paris.

She passed through the dress department, noting that there were lots of summer clothes on the sale racks now. The autumn stocks were already taking over, despite the weather. She paused as she saw a particularly pretty dress, and it was just her size. Oh well, she thought, I may as well try it on. Perhaps this would be better than a hat, after all.

She had to admit it was. It fitted her perfectly and matched her colouring exactly. The dress could have been made for her. Without thinking twice, she made for the sales desk. There was just one woman in front of her, but she seemed to be having some sort of argument with the saleslady.

"I think you should refund my money," she was saying. "This is the dress I want. That one doesn't fit."

"Why didn't you try it on before you bought it, madam?" It seemed a reasonable question to Dilys.

"Because I didn't have time. Now, once and for all, can you exchange this dress for this one?"

While the altercation was going on, Dilys observed the customer who was obviously standing her ground on the principle that she was 'always right'. Dilys thought she was being rather unreasonable, and she didn't like the way she was talking to the poor saleswoman.

She had to admit, though, she had pretty hair. A lovely auburn colour, wound into a fashionable knot. She couldn't see the woman's face as she had her back to her, but she could see she was well dressed and slim. Probably very pretty, surmised Dilys. The pretty ones always think they have a God-given right to throw their weight about, she thought.

At last, they seemed to be coming to a compromise, which was just as well, as she was almost prepared to return the dress to the rack and go and have a coffee somewhere. Her feet were beginning to ache, as she had been standing for quite a while, and the heat was oppressive. Maybe a cool milkshake would be better than a coffee. Oh yes, and a Danish pastry.

"So, you'll take this dress back and have this one altered, will you?" the pretty auburn-haired lady was saying.

"Of course, madam."

"And you'll send this to my home address when it is ready?"

"Yes, madam. Will you write your address here, please?"

"There you are," said the woman. Dilys watched her hand the piece of paper back to the salesgirl with a flourish. "That's where to send it. It will be delivered during the day, won't it?"

"Naturally, madam," said the salesgirl. Dilys could see she was puzzled by this question. So was Dilys. After all, when did the Post Office ever deliver anything when you were actually in to receive it?

"Can I have your name, please?" the salesgirl was asking now.

"Yes. It's Mrs Pearl Carmichael …."

Dilys stepped away from the queue that was now forming behind her. *Mrs Pearl Carmichael*. It was possible there was more than one woman with that name, but she knew this was Barney's wife. He had shown her a picture of her once, and there was no doubt. It was her. And there was no wheelchair to be seen anywhere.

50

Barney sat on at his desk staring into space after Tony Halliday had left. He was worried. Poor Muriel was about to get the third degree and it was all his fault. Halliday had told Barney he was thinking of something to charge her with, but was eventually dissuaded to do so. But Halliday had still been out for blood. It seemed that Ted Randall's incarceration wasn't nearly enough for all the trouble he had been put to.

Then there had been the question of a formal identification of the body, once known as Leon Conrad but who was really just plain old Derek Baker, apparently. What were the legal implications of that muddle? Halliday had wanted to know. He had been placated by Barney telling him about his client, Mrs Jeanne Conrad, who had claimed to be Leon's mother.

"So, I suppose I should charge her with kidnapping, then, shouldn't I?" Halliday had said.

Barney had demurred at this. "Should you?"

"No, probably not. The crime didn't take place on my patch. Ergo, not my problem." Halliday had convinced himself. Barney hadn't wanted any convincing, thinking she would probably suffer enough now that Leon was dead.

"Anyway, she's your best bet for a formal identification," Barney had told the Inspector.

That had sent the Inspector off happily. He was to make a detour to the home of Muriel Bird, leaving Barney with the dubious pleasure of warning Mrs

Conrad that a visit from the police was imminent. She would, by now, have seen the papers anyway, and God knew what she was making of them.

He set off, finally, for Claridges for what promised to be a very trying interview. In his pocket was her unbanked cheque which he planned, very reluctantly, to return to her. There was no way he could accept money from someone guilty of kidnapping, now, could he?

He had never set foot in Claridges before. Nor the Ritz, nor the Savoy, come to that. They were a different world to him. He was treated with deference by the desk clerk who was a world away from the likes of Ted Randall, or at least Barney supposed so, not having met the man. But this clerk was politeness itself. He was asked to wait in the cocktail lounge while he called Mrs Conrad on the internal telephone. She was in her room, he had assured Barney. That didn't fill him with joy, either. He was half hoping she would be out, but it would only delay the inevitable. He reminded himself, too, that he had to treat her with kid gloves for, whatever the rights and wrongs of the matter, she had lost the 'son' she had brought up and cared for for over twenty years.

Mrs Conrad soon appeared before him and he stood awkwardly, holding out his hand for her to shake. She ignored it and sat down opposite him. She raised an eyebrow and a waiter was instantly at her side. She ordered a dry martini, a very dry martini.

"Do you want anything?" she asked Barney, obviously as an afterthought. Her question couldn't have been less gracious if she'd tried.

"Er, no, thanks," he said, longing for a cold beer.

"I – I came to see how you were," said Barney, when she had her dry (very) martini in front of her.

"As you can see," she said, sipping her drink with elegance. He had to give her her due. She was certainly a dignified woman, considering the circumstances. Mind you, he thought, she didn't seem that upset over the death of Leon Conrad, at least not as upset as he expected her to be.

"Yes," he agreed.

"I've seen the news, Mr Carmichael," she said quietly. Her eyebrow was raised again, and before he'd had time to register the fact, there was another martini in front of her.

"I – I came as soon as I reasonably could," he said.

"Thank you for that. But it is little comfort." She took out a miniscule lace hanky and dabbed her dry (very) eyes with it. "I trusted you. I thought you would find my son."

"Except he wasn't your son, was he, Mrs Conrad?"

She bristled visibly at this. "I reared that boy for twenty-two years. He was my son in all but birth."

"You stole him from his real mother who committed suicide because of it."

"I – I regret that. I never knew."

"It wouldn't have changed anything though, would it? Even if you'd known, you couldn't give him back to her, could you? She was dead."

She looked abashed now. Discomfited. She wriggled her long legs into a more comfortable position. A third martini was now produced courtesy of the raised eyebrow.

"Anyway, I came to return your cheque," said Barney, pleased that he had made her squirm. It seemed he had the moral high ground now. "I don't think it right I should take it – in the circumstances."

"As you please," she said. She left it on the table where he had placed it. "I was very unhappy, you know. When I took Leon. I'd just lost my own son in a car crash, along with my husband. I wasn't thinking straight. All I knew was that I had to have that little boy. He looked so much like my Zachary –"

"Zachary?"

"My boy. He looked so like my little Zach, I thought he would make me happy. But he didn't. He wasn't my son. But I lavished everything on him, everything money could buy. He wanted for nothing. He had a better life than his real mother could ever have given him."

He watched as she took out a cigarette holder from her handbag and proceeded to place a cigarette in it. The ever-vigilant waiter was there with a lighter.

"Now he's dead too," stated Barney quietly.

"Yes."

"He took revenge for his mother."

"Revenge?"

"Yes. Those women he murdered used to work with her. They taunted her when she lost her little boy. Blamed her for not looking after him properly. Drove her to hang herself."

"That's why he did it? It doesn't say that in the papers. In fact, they offer no explanation at all for the killing spree."

"That will come out in time, Mrs Conrad, I'm sure."

"Well, I want to thank you for telling me that. It gives me some comfort to know he wasn't a complete psycho."

Barney, in his opinion, thought Leon Conrad was almost as complete a psycho as anyone Alfred Hitchcock could have dreamed up, but he didn't say so. Complete psycho or not, here was a woman who was suffering bereavement and he couldn't forget Muriel either. She'd been bereaved too. The whole thing was a mess and he didn't have the heart to apportion blame, even if he knew where to start.

"I think I ought to tell you, Mrs Conrad, that the police will require a formal identification of the body. And, as you knew him better than anyone, I'm afraid you will have to do that."

Her face went white. "But won't he be all broken up? Gee, I don't have to look at him like that, do I?"

"I'm afraid you do, Mrs Conrad, I'm sorry."

He wasn't sorry, however. She deserved to see the bashed up, broken remains of Leon Conrad. It would do her good to see where her one rash, criminal act of twenty-two years ago had led.

51

It had been a long day for Barney, and about to get even longer. It was time to return home to Pearl, but he was back in his office instead. He opened a can of lager and undid his tie. He went to the window and gazed up at the sky. It was no longer blue. In fact, there was no blue anywhere. A pall of grey cloud hung over everything, matching his mood exactly. The weather was about to break at last.

His head throbbed and he searched in his drawer for some aspirin to take with his lager. The thought of going back to Pearl only made his headache worse. In the distance, a rumble of thunder could be heard. He rubbed his sore temples and felt like crying.

But what had he to be so unhappy about? he asked himself. Jim was going to be all right and would be home tomorrow. Daisy had gone through with her 'procedure' and he was collecting her early tomorrow morning. He mentally ticked things off. The charlady murders had been solved and so had the Conrad case. Tick, tick.

Mrs Conrad was a cold, calculating woman, he had no doubt about that. She wouldn't be the type to faint at the sight of a bloodied corpse, not even of her own son. Only he wasn't her son, had never been her son, and now wouldn't be anybody's son, ever again. Tick, tick. The only thing left to deal with was Pearl. It wasn't so bad, really.

Then he thought about Dilys. How different he would be feeling now if he was going home to her instead of to Pearl. He swallowed the aspirin and swigged the lager. He could feel the cold liquid go down his windpipe. It was a comforting sensation. The thunder was growing louder now.

Suddenly the phone leapt into life, startling him. It was gone seven o'clock. Clients shouldn't be ringing at this time, he thought crossly. Did they think he'd no home to go to? Even if that home had only Pearl in it, and not even a nice cat or dog to greet him. They didn't know that, did they?

He'd a good mind not to answer it. Let them leave a message on the new-fangled answering machine that only Muriel knew how to work.

But then, he thought, if it was a paying client, could he afford not to answer it? Besides, it would delay his return home. He picked it up.

"Barney?"

It was a female voice, one he knew well. His headache seemed to vanish as he heard the familiar tones.

"Dilys?"

"Thank goodness. You're still there. I didn't want to ring you at home."

"No, no. Please, never do that."

"I wouldn't – only I might have done this evening if you hadn't answered."

"What do you mean?"

"Barney, I want you to do what I say and not to ask any questions. Okay?"

Barney was puzzled. He had never heard her sound so determined. Sweetly determined, he adjusted. She could never be anything but sweet to him.

"Er – why?"

"Just say that you'll do as I say without asking questions."

"All right, Dilys. I'm too tired to argue."

"Good. First, don't go home. Do not pass go, do not collect two hundred pounds – " She was giggling.

"Dilys, have you been drinking?"

"Not yet."

"You said 'don't go home'?"

"That's right."

"But I have to."

"No, you don't. Not yet."

"Okay." Barney smiled into the receiver as if she could see him. He didn't mind agreeing to that.

"Now, when you leave the office go into the off licence and pick up a bottle of that wine you brought round last time."

"Wine? Why should I buy wine? What's going on, Dilys? I love you to bits, but I think you've got a touch of the sun."

"No. I'm completely rational. I'm seeing things clearly for the first time in ages. I love you to bits, too."

Barney felt like dancing around the office and singing. He did neither. He still couldn't believe what he was hearing. "Darling," he began.

"Shut up, Barney," she said abruptly. "Now just get into your car and come round here. As quickly as you can."

"Come to you? Now?"

"Yes. Now."

"But – but – "

"Stop butting, are you a goat? Just come. I'll explain everything when I see you. Oh, and you'd better buy a toothbrush on your way over."

He put the receiver down. What was she saying? He couldn't misinterpret that, surely? A toothbrush?

He wandered out of the office, into the lift and out into the street in a daze. As he came out of the off licence, he felt the first drops of rain on his face.

21686493R00174

Printed in Poland
by Amazon Fulfillment
Poland Sp. z o.o., Wrocław